Free to Deceive
A Katie Freeman Mystery

Julie Mellon

COPYRIGHT

Text Copyright © 2015 Julie Mellon
All Rights Reserved
Cover art and design by Ryan Bukowski

All rights reserved. This book or any portion thereof may not be reproduced or used in any manner whatsoever without the express written permission of the publisher or author, except for the use of brief quotations in a book review. The story contained within is a work of fiction. Names and characters are the product of the author's imagination and any resemblance to actual person's living or dead, is entirely coincidental.

ISBN: 978-1512256550 (print)
ISBN: 978-0-9862997-3-5(ebook)

To those who inspire me daily to pursue my dreams.

Other books by
Julie Mellon

Katie Freeman
Free to Kill
Free to Deceive

Tip of the Spear
In the Shadows

A Word from the Author

Welcome back to another Katie Freeman Mystery! Thank you so much for the wonderful feedback on Katie's debut novel. I am having so much fun writing her story.

In this book Katie and Michael tackle the ever-increasing problem of hate-crimes and I tried to represent the stereotypes and discrimination faced by the LGBTQ community in as sensitive a manner as possible. Please, take a minute to search out those you love and give them a hug, regardless of how they live their lives. You never know when they might not be there anymore.

A big thank you to Lyndsey Godwin who took the time to walk through the numerous issues faced by the LGBTQ community. Without her assistance, I wouldn't have been able to present the viewpoints of the various characters.

Another big thank you to my beta readers Sarah Ross – for ripping it apart before putting it back together; Laura Haines – for telling me when something is lacking; and Michelle Bukowski – for not only giving her opinions, but also for keeping me inline and online. Without your role this book wouldn't be what it is now. To Mike Spring, thank you again for your wonderful editing skills – I hope this was more enjoyable than the textbooks you were slogging through.

Now, turn the page and enjoy Free to Deceive!

5

One

Katie Freeman stood looking down at the hole in the ground trying to keep her mind on the bodies being unearthed instead of on the secret she was keeping from her partner. The spring rains that usually overshadowed middle Tennessee in April had made a reappearance in late June. The air was chilly and the cold mist that constantly fell from the sky made everything feel damp. Katie didn't remember the last time she felt dry or warm and it had to do with more than the uncharacteristic weather.

On the ground around her were the dead and dying narcissus flowers that the crew from the medical examiner's office had dug up three days ago when the first body had been reported. *If you ignore the police, the coroner's van, and the body bags piling up, this is a beautiful spot.* Katie took a few minutes to glance around. She and her partner were huddled under a tarp canopy, one of many that had been erected around the statue of Nemesis that stood sentry over the pond.

Three days ago, the local police department received a call from the groundskeeper of Smyrna Park, a scant two-square-mile park located on the southern edge of Smyrna, Tennessee. The West Fork Stones River flowed lazily nearby; one of the underground tunnels it had burrowed erupted through the soil to form the small body of water known as West Fork Pond. As the town of

Julie Mellon

Smyrna grew and houses began to encroach on the river, the city took measures to protect as much green space as possible. The result was the creation of Smyrna Park, which included the pond and surrounding grassy areas. The park became a popular gathering area for the neighborhoods that sprang up and in the intervening twelve years the residents made improvements to it, adding walking and bike trails, benches, pavilions, playground areas, landscaping and sculptures.

A statue of Nemesis, the Greek god of retribution, had been erected at the water's edge. One of the myths of Nemesis was that she had punished Narcissus for his treatment of Echo. Narcissus was a hunter renowned for his beauty. He was loved by Echo, but spurned her love until the only thing that remained of her was the sound of her cry echoing through the night. Narcissus was said to have been punished by falling in love with his own reflection in a pond, where he eventually drowned. The sculpture had been placed as if Nemesis were keeping watch over the pond to ensure Narcissus didn't return. Ironically, the landscaping around the statue of Nemesis was a bed of narcissus flowers. A small plaque at the bottom of the statue was engraved with: *If there is a single quality that is shared by all great men, it is vanity. —Yousef Karsh.*

The groundskeeper had been going about his day checking the

Free to Deceive

landscaping and evaluating the need to dig up and replant the various areas. Approaching the pond, he noticed that the narcissi planted around the statue had been disturbed. Thinking some of the neighborhood children had been up to no good, he made his way over to straighten up the damage and salvage as many of the bulbs as he could. As he used his hand to form a hole in the loose dirt so he could bury the roots of one of the displaced plants, his fingers brushed against something firm. Expecting to see a rock, or perhaps even a dog bone, he dug a little further to toss the item out of the flowerbed. Grabbing a firm hold on the object, he gave a small tug and came away holding the fingers of a buried hand. He gave a small shout as he stumbled backward a few steps, still in a squat, and landed on his butt a short distance away.

The local police had shown up in response to the groundskeeper's call and began the process of exhuming the remains. The coroner spent several hours sifting through the soil and finally revealed the body of a male in his early-to-mid-twenties. A body bag was brought over and, with the help of an assistant, the male was lifted and zipped into it. The coroner stood and began brushing the dirt off his knees when his gaze came to rest on the spot where he had been kneeling. He bent back over, brushed aside the dirt, and came face-to-face with another finger. His curse was followed by a peal of thunder and the beginning of the rain that had yet to let up, three days later.

When the third and partially skeletonized body had been discovered, Detective Thomas, a local officer, had called in the FBI. Katie Freeman and her partner, Michael Powell, arrived on scene at two in the afternoon to the sound of rain beating down on tarps strung between poles that had been sunk into the soil surrounding the statue. Marie Bennett, the FBI medical examiner, had arrived shortly behind them and the transfer of the process of exhumation began. Lightning and rain forced them to call a stop to the recovery at six the first day. The total body count had been five.

Day two began with the discovery of a sixth body and ended with the recovery of a tenth. And still the rain came down in steady sheets. The temperature for the day was fifty-eight - - unusually low for middle Tennessee in late June.

Day three rolled around and the rain had finally slowed to a mist that seeped into Katie's clothing even worse than the downpour. At least when the sheets of rain had been coming down she could stand under the canopy and stay relatively dry. The mist hung in the air and blew in all directions with the smallest breeze, burrowing into any and all clothing and hair in its path. She stood next to Michael with a cup of hot cocoa in her hands trying to warm them as they watched Dr. Bennett uncover the eleventh body.

"You're very quiet today," Michael said. "Something on your mind? Are you still thinking about Downing?" Michael had sensed Katie's preoccupation for the past several weeks, since their last case ended with the perpetrator committing suicide practically in front of them. He had thought that if he gave Katie time she would open up to him. So far that hadn't happened. With nothing to do in this investigation until they had a starting point, Michael decided to press Katie for some answers. If she couldn't handle the outcome of a case that ended badly he needed to know.

Katie had transferred to the Tennessee office almost two months earlier and was paired with Michael, whose former partner had retired. Michael was immediately impressed with the way her mind worked and how she was easily able to read people. They had developed a rhythm in their investigation that worked to accentuate both their strengths. For a while, he fought an attraction to her, but quickly came to realize that she was more like an additional sister, someone he was protective of. At least, he was trying to convince himself that was all there was to it. Since he had four sisters, he was well versed in being

Julie Mellon

protective.

    Because he hadn't known her long, he didn't know how she handled death, especially one so close in proximity. She had seemed fine during the few days after Downing had taken his own life rather than be arrested, but once they had finalized the paperwork, she began to withdraw. It was fine with him if she needed time to process what had happened, but Michael needed to know how to handle the post-case wrap-up with his new partner.

    Katie took a sip of her hot cocoa and ran her hand over her dark hair, which was pulled back in her customary bun before answering. "Of course not," she said. "I haven't given him a second thought since we walked in that room and his brains were on the wall. He deserved a worse punishment but at least he saved the taxpayers the cost of a trial and housing him for the rest of his life." She was relieved that Michael had added a direct question to his comment; she didn't like keeping secrets and was a terrible liar. By bringing up Downing, she was able to ignore the guilt stabbing at her insides when she thought about what she had discovered the weekend before last. Why had she ever gone to see Billy Sheppard? Now that she knew the truth about who she was - - and more importantly who her mother was - - how was she supposed to concentrate on her job? And what would happen to her career once everyone found out? She loved what she

Free to Deceive

did for a living and she was making friends with her new coworkers, a first for her with her social awkwardness. Now she just felt like she was betraying them all. Katie forced herself to stop dwelling on that situation and focus on the one in front of her. "How many bodies do you think are out here?"

The ring of bodies now extended halfway around the small pond. They had been buried face down with their arms outstretched, linked finger to finger. Katie pictured a string of paper people like she used to cut out of a single sheet of paper when she was a kid — linked at the hands and feet. Only in this instance, the feet were crossed at the ankle, and just the hands touched. Dr. Bennett stood and stretched before making her way to the canopy where Katie and Michael stood. She pulled off a set of non-latex sterile gloves and reached for a cup of coffee. "Eleven is uncovered," she said. "Found the link to twelve. They've been progressively more decomposed as we've moved around the circle. I can tell you that they all appear to be male — early twenties to early thirties. Aside from that, we'll have to wait until I have them back in the lab and on my table. I sure hope this is the last one. I don't think my back can take being hunched over for many more hours." She took a sip of coffee and accepted a croissant with ham, egg and cheese that one of her assistants passed over to her.

Julie Mellon

"Is there anything you can give us to go on that would help us get started on identifying any of the victims?" Katie was anxious to have something to focus on. Keeping busy gave her mind less time to wander.

"There isn't much to go on. All of the bodies are naked. There isn't so much as a leftover button in the graves. The first body we discovered reminds me of the missing kid from Murfreesboro, the one that went missing early last week. The rate of decomposition on the body supports that length of time for approximate date of death. I only had a brief look at the body, though, so don't quote me on that. There isn't enough of his skin left to get prints, so if you want a place to start, how about getting me dental records to match that case?" At nearly sixty, Dr. Bennett's reference to the missing "kid" was actually a twenty-four year old male student at Middle Tennessee State University, known as MTSU.

"I remember hearing about that disappearance," Michael said. "What makes you think the first body could be his?"

Smyrna was only fifteen miles from Murfreesboro, and given that the bodies had been found on the southern side of the city, it was even closer. The possibility of this being the missing student was completely plausible, especially because the last place the man had been spotted was on his way to work in The

Free to Deceive

Avenue, a large shopping center less than ten miles away. He worked as a server at one of the steakhouses there. His roommate had told police that he left the house they shared shortly before four-thirty so he could be at work to start his shift at five. His car was found in the lot of the restaurant where he worked, but he never clocked in for his shift. Beyond that, Michael's knowledge of the case was limited to what had been reported on the news.

"The general height and build of the body matches the description, as does the hair color and length. I recalled the picture on the news showing a guy with shoulder-length hair that was naturally wavy. Any woman would kill for hair like that. Anyway, it's just a guess, but it's something for you to do and will help me get started once I finally get out of this damn rain." She pulled a fresh pair of gloves from her bag and set out to exhume body number twelve.

"We already have Lucy and Andy searching for missing males in the area," Katie said, referring to two of their coworkers who generally worked sex crimes, especially internet and child pornography. They enjoyed being given cases that let them step away from the scum of the earth for a while. "Let's see if we can touch base with the detective in charge of this disappearance."

Julie Mellon

Two

Katie called the Murfreesboro police to find the contact information for the detective in charge while Michael started the car. She immediately adjusted the vents so that the stream of heat blasted straight on her. "Who ever heard of having to use the heat in June in Tennessee?" Her grumbling was met with a small chuckle from Michael, but he adjusted the dual temperature controls so that her side was warmer. The thoughtful action threatened to bring back the guilt she had been holding at bay. Her thoughts were cut short when Detective Sheila Reynolds picked up the phone at the other end. After explaining the situation, Detective Reynolds agreed to meet them at the restaurant where the missing student worked.

The drive to the steakhouse passed in comfortable silence with only the occasional outburst of singing from Michael when one of his favorite classic rock songs came on the radio. A tall, attractive African-American woman was waiting under the awning over the front door of the restaurant and ushered them inside.

"Please call me Sheila," she said upon introduction. Katie couldn't help but notice the appreciative glance the other woman cast over Michael — she had grown used to that reaction from women, and sometimes even men, since they were partnered together. She had to admit that Michael was beyond good looking at over six feet tall with dark hair and the deepest brown eyes she had ever seen, and in his dark purple shirt under a silvery gray suit jacket he looked even better. She had been attracted to him when they first became partners, but her rules against dating coworkers had relegated him to non-dating material. She was happy with the decision and it made it easier to find humor in all the women throwing themselves at him, even if she hadn't yet worked up the courage to tease him about it.

They were shown to a large circular table in the corner of the restaurant. Katie took the seat in the corner with Michael to her left. Sheila took the chair one seat over to Katie's right. All three had a line-of-sight to the main dining area of the restaurant with two empty seats remaining.

Once they were seated, Sheila pulled out the file containing the history of the investigation into the disappearance of Franklin Newberry and passed it across the table. "There really isn't much to go on here. The guy literally disappeared into thin air. We looked at traffic cameras between his house and here. He stopped at a few traffic lights, appeared to be singing along to the radio. He was alone in the car. The last shot we have of him is when he turned off the main road into the parking lot of the building where he worked. The

Free to Deceive

restaurant doesn't have cameras in the back parking lot where employees are instructed to park. No one remembers seeing him pull in. There were two additional servers who were arriving for the same shift; the first doesn't remember seeing his car in the lot, but the second one does. She said his car was parked in the spot next to the one she pulled into, but he was nowhere around. Management attempted to call his cell phone but received no answer. They walked out to his car once the other server reported seeing it in the lot. His phone was located in the center console."

Sheila paused as the waitress arrived with their drinks and took their order. Katie took her advice and ordered the broccoli and cheese soup, which was made with asiago cheese. Before they finished ordering, two men in suits strolled up and pulled out the chairs on either side of Detective Reynolds. They added their orders before the waitress left.

"Dane Crawford, Special Agent." The reddish-blond man who sat between Sheila and Katie extended his hand to Katie with a rakish smile. Katie's first impression was that he was cocky and overconfident. Her next thought was that his scruffy, haven't-shaved-yet-today look was his way of thumbing his nose at the rules. His tan suit, white shirt and cerulean blue tie looked good against his golden tan skin and blue eyes. He knew he looked good and he wasn't afraid to use it to his advantage. She couldn't help but feel he was flirting with her.

"Special Agent Michael Powell," Michael interjected, reaching across Katie to take the man's hand. His introduction was unnecessary; Michael had worked with Dane on several prior cases. There was no love lost between the two. The office rumor mill attributed it to the two men both being so attractive. Everyone thought the two were in a competition to see who could get the most female attention. But the truth was that Michael thought Dane used his looks to get by and that his investigations took second place to his arrogance. "Pompous" was the word that came to mind when Michael thought of Dane.

Dane took his eyes off Katie to look at Michael. "Well, well, if it isn't Mr. Colorful. Nice tie today." He smirked as he dismissed Michael's presence and returned his attention to Katie. "What's your name, darlin'?"

"Special Agent Katie Freeman," Katie replied in a clipped tone, finally extending her hand in return. When Dane took it, she made sure her grip was firm and she never broke eye contact. His attitude toward Michael had completely reinforced her opinion of him.

"What brings you here?" Michael asked. His abruptness was so out of line with his normal personality that Katie made a mental note to find out about the history between these two.

"I called them in," Sheila answered. "This is Special Agent Ryan Brewer. They've been consulting on this case for a few days."

"Why call in the FBI for a missing persons case? We usually only step in if you suspect a kidnapping." Katie was the one who asked the question. Michael didn't bother trying to soften her approach as he usually did. He was still too annoyed that Dane was at the table.

Sheila reached into her briefcase and brought out two additional files. "When the Newberry kid went missing ten days ago, alarms started going off in my head. I've been working on two other missing persons cases over the last year and a half that involve men in this age range. Missing kids and missing females are normal in my world. But three men in the same age range who disappeared off the face of the earth for no apparent reason in the span of a few months was so out of the ordinary that I thought they might be connected. I contacted the FBI last week and met with Ryan and Dane two days ago. When you contacted me today, I called to see if they would join us."

Reaching across the table, Katie grabbed the folders and passed one to Michael. The table was quiet as the two read through the papers. As they were finishing, the waitress

Julie Mellon

appeared and delivered their food.

They waited until she left before resuming their conversation. Katie picked up her spoon and took a bite of her soup. It smelled heavenly and the first bite began warming her up from the inside.

"So Josh McDaniel disappeared in January. Single, MTSU student, twenty-two, worked in a sporting goods store here in this shopping center. No known enemies, just didn't show up for work one day." Katie summarized her file and looked to Michael for the information contained in the one he was reading.

"Daniel King, twenty-three, single, worked in the bookstore two stores down from here. No known enemies, just didn't show up for work one day last March, a little over a year ago. I agree, these have an eerily similar theme."

"There's more," Sheila said. "All three of their cars were found behind the stores where they worked. Also, I believe all three were homosexual." All four sets of eyes looked at her as she dropped the last bit of information.

"You never told us that." Dane's chest puffed out with indignation at not having all the facts.

"You didn't hang around long enough to hear me out on what I had learned. Besides, I'm not 100% certain on them being homosexual. I know for a fact that Josh was. He was out of the closet and open about his orientation. His family was supportive, but he did experience rejection from some of his long-time friends. Daniel is a little more difficult. He was a loner who didn't seem to have many friends. Those that claim to know him describe him as quiet and bookish. He was prone to depression. I actually haven't found anyone he dated, so my assumptions stem from the information I found on his laptop. He frequented websites that were homosexual in nature, but all his social media is devoid of personal opinions or posts. If he was gay, he kept it buried.

"As for Franklin Newberry, he's a twenty-four year old who lives with another man. His roommate, Sam Blackstone, is openly homosexual. Franklin's family claims he was straight, but I think he went to great lengths to hide his true self from them. The house where Franklin and Sam live is set up with two rooms that are made up as if they each had their own individual space. But if you look closely, one room is definitely not used. Also, Franklin's family calls him Frankie, which is the name he grew up using. In college, he had his friends call him Franklin, as if he were trying to distance himself from his past. His family is devoutly Southern Baptist and would not accept his lifestyle. I think this bears further investigation."

Both Michael and Katie were impressed with the deductive

reasoning Sheila used. As she talked, they watched Dane scowl at her opinions. Michael knew Dane was a chauvinist, and he relished the idea that there were two women at the table who were better investigators than Dane. Looking at Katie as Sheila wrapped up her speech, he nodded at her to take the lead. Katie had the attitude to put Dane in his place.

"I like your reasoning," she began. "I think we should find time to talk to Sam Blackstone privately, without Franklin's family present. What have you two found in the past few days?" Katie asked, directing a challenging gaze at Dane. Up until this point Dane's partner had remained silent.

"We haven't found any missing gays," Dane said bluntly.

Ryan decided to come to his partner's rescue. "We found twenty-two additional males, ages twenty to thirty-five, missing in the last five years from across the state. I don't recall there being a mention of any of them being homosexual, but we weren't narrowing our search by that criteria." He pulled the files from his briefcase and laid them on the table. Ryan's manner was calm and observant. He had the lean build of a runner and looked as if he harnessed a lot of energy. He sat still in his seat, but his eyes constantly roamed the restaurant watching all the people and movements going on around him.

Katie noticed that Ryan chose the chair that faced the

room, whereas his partner sat with his back to the others in the restaurant, as if he hadn't a care in the world. It was unusual for anyone in law enforcement to sit with their back to the room and Katie had to again wonder at the amount of arrogance Dane possessed. She immediately warmed to Ryan and wondered how he managed to work with Dane on a daily basis.

Sheila, Michael and Katie each took a file and began leafing through them. They sat in silence for several long minutes as the files were exchanged and their plates cleared from the table. Once all the files had been glanced over, the five of them began debating the merits of each and whether there was a thread that connected any more of them to the three Sheila had been investigating.

In the end, it was decided that Katie, Michael and Sheila would interview Sam Blackstone while Ryan and Dane began the process of requesting dental records for the twenty-two files they had gathered. Sheila already had dental records on the cases she was handling.

Three

Katie and Michael followed Sheila to a small house within walking distance of MTSU's campus. It was weathered gray with black shutters and white trim. The yard was neatly maintained and yellow lilies were in bloom along the front. A man opened the door and led them to a small living room with dark brown leather furniture. Sitting on the couch was Sam Blackstone, his mid-length blonde hair with highlighted tips standing in stark contrast to the pallor of his skin. His red-rimmed green eyes were dull and filled with pain. When he saw Detective Reynolds, he attempted to pull himself together.

"Don't," Sheila said in sympathy. She sat next to him and laid her hand on his arm. "You don't have to pretend for us. We know, and it's okay."

At her words, Sam broke down in heaving sobs and buried his face in his hands. The man who let them in sat down on his other side and wrapped his arms around Sam, rocking him while he let his tears out.

"I'm sorry. This has been a difficult week. I can't figure out where he is or why he left. Have you discovered anything?" The anguish Sam felt came through in his tone.

"Sam, these are Special Agents with the FBI. I've asked them to step in on this case for various reasons. But first, I think you should know that we think we've found Franklin."

"Oh, God. He's all right. Please tell me he's okay." Sam gripped both Sheila's hands as he pleaded with her, his face changing from gray to white.

"I'm sorry, Sam, but we recovered a body three days ago that we think is Franklin." Sheila was gentle with her tone, but her words left no room for misinterpretation. She didn't want to give him any false hope that they had made a mistake.

As Sam once again broke down, Sheila looked to the agents communicating that they should take over.

Once Sam's tears had slowed, Michael took over the questions. "I'm sorry for your loss, Sam. We haven't positively identified the body, or notified his next of kin, but we feel confident that the man we recovered is Franklin Newberry. The description matched, as did the timeframe for his death. We wouldn't be here if we weren't confident that the person we found is Franklin."

Again, they waited until Sam composed himself. When he was able to speak, he asked, "How did he die?"

"We don't know yet. The medical examiner hasn't completed an autopsy yet. Franklin's body is one of thirteen that have been uncovered so far." They had received a text from Dr. Bennett as they were leaving the restaurant that the thirteenth

Julie Mellon

body had been uncovered with no additional ones linked to it. She was leaving the scene to go to the lab and begin the process of autopsying the ones that had been recovered, but she left her assistants and a few officers to do a search for any additional bodies that might have been missed.

"You're talking about those bodies in Smyrna that they've been digging up the past few days?" This question came from the man who had let them in.

"And you are…?" Katie asked.

"Oh, I'm Robert Ellwood. You can call me Robbie. I've been friends with Sam and Franklin for years."

Seeming satisfied with the explanation, Michael continued. "Yes, we're talking about the bodies in Smyrna. We aren't ready to release any information to the press, and like I said, we haven't made a positive identification or notified Franklin's family. So, for now, we ask that anything we discuss today remain confidential."

Both men nodded and Sam said, "We're experts at keeping secrets. Sometimes it's the only way to survive."

This time it was Katie that picked up the conversation. "Sam, we've identified a total of twenty-four other males between the ages of twenty and thirty-five that have gone missing in the past five years. Of those, at least two were homosexual. While we don't know if those two are part of they thirteen we've recovered, we are trying to get a jump-start on this investigation and see if there is a possibility that this might be a hate crime. Can you think of anyone who might want to hurt Franklin? Have there been any threats to him lately?"

Sam was shaking his head long before Katie finished. "Franklin is the straightest-acting guy I've ever met." He chuckled as he thought of Franklin. "His family makes him behave that way. He hasn't been able to overcome the fear of being rejected by them. I'm the one who's open about myself. But when we're in public, I respect his choice to remain in the closet. It gets tiring sometimes, having to live a lie. But I love him."

The three law enforcement agents noticed the use of present tense when Sam talked about Franklin. This was typical behavior for someone who recently found out a loved one died. It was also a good gauge to see if that person had committed murder -- in those cases, the murderer would have had time to adjust their thinking to past tense -- a dead giveaway to their guilt. The three of them looked at each other, silently acknowledging their agreement that Sam was not the person responsible for killing Franklin.

"Sam, would you mind if we looked through Franklin's things? It would really help if we could see his actual belongings, not the staged room you showed me last time." Sheila was gentle in her question, but direct enough to let Sam know she had caught on to the ploy the last time she was there.

"Is that how you knew we were a couple?"

"That's part of it. Cops can tell when a person is hiding something. I spent a few days investigating you thinking you might have had something to do with his disappearance. I knew you were hiding some facts from me. But when I discovered you were openly gay, I started thinking about the house and how it was arranged. The pictures of the two of you on vacation, Franklin's room with a layer of dust on the bedspread, none of it added up until I rearranged your relationship."

"Well, I suppose it's a good thing his family never came over. They didn't like me -- always told Franklin that I was a bad influence and that he should be careful about anything I said. They even warned him that I would make advances toward him and to lock his door at night so I couldn't come in and rape him. It was so hard on him to live with their hate. We met when he was eighteen and a freshman at MTSU and have been inseparable for six years. He was almost finished with his Master's degree and was planning on becoming a teacher. We were so close to getting everything we've worked for all these years."

As Sam broke down again, Robbie waved the officers toward

the back of the house, indicating that they could go search as they wished. Sheila led the way to the bedroom at the far end of the hall.

"I searched the other room last time I was here. There are off-season clothes hanging in the closet, but the summer clothes are all in here. That was clue number one that the room wasn't used. The closets are small and with two of them needing the space, it appears they alternate the wardrobes by season."

The three of them silently went through the bedroom and the small attached bath, as well as the hall bath before making their way back into the living room.

"Did Franklin have a computer?"

Sam was drinking a glass of water. He nodded, stood up and walked to the other side of the living room where a small desk stood tucked under the front window. He picked up a laptop and returned, handing it to Katie. They talked for a few more minutes before the three left Sam to his grief, with a parting word to remind him of the need to keep this quiet for a little longer.

That evening, Michael dropped Katie off at the Bed and Breakfast that she still called home. Michael's sister and her family ran it, though he had neglected to tell her this when he recommended that she stay there. Every time she debated moving out she would think of all the home-cooked meals that she would miss and how she had gotten so attached to the family's three kids. Michael's sister, Caroline, had become a very close friend as well. For now, she saw no reason to move, so she continued to pay her board and grow more attached to the family. Living there also helped alleviate the loneliness that had been present since she left her mother's house at eighteen. Just as quickly as her mother came to mind, she pushed the thought away. Lately, Katie became angry every time she thought of her. The sense of betrayal was overwhelming.

"I'm going to run the dental x-rays up to Dr. Bennett. Should I pick you up in the morning?" When they were first partners, he started picking her up without asking which made her angry. He was just trying to give her time to learn her way around, but she thought he was being chauvinistic. Now, Michael always asked if he should pick her up.

"Do you want me to run to Nashville and drop them off?" Katie didn't want to seem as if she weren't pulling her weight in the partnership.

"Nah, I'm picking up Candice and taking her to dinner in Nashville, so I'm headed that way anyway. She won't mind the detour." The last part wasn't true; Candice hated anything to do with Michael's work. At first he thought that was a good thing -- it forced him to let go of work when they were together. Then he realize that it caused issues with communication because she was never willing to listen when he needed to talk and she never understood the strange hours the job sometimes required. She also had a problem with his new partner - apparently a beautiful woman wasn't someone she wanted Michael to get out of bed for in the middle of the night. It didn't matter that the only thing he was doing with that beautiful woman was standing over dead bodies.

"I thought you two broke up?" During their investigation of the missing women last month, Katie had seen the blonde bombshell stalk off after an argument with Michael. He hadn't wanted to tell Katie what it was about, which had hurt her feelings and brought to her attention the attraction she felt. He finally let it slip that Candice was a girlfriend in a relationship that was going bad. Katie had stamped out her attraction before it could grow any further, but not before having several discussions with Michael's sister, Caroline, about the woman. Apparently his family didn't like her any more than Katie did -- and Katie had never actually met her.

"I thought so too, but she isn't ready to let go."

"You know, you need to stop being such a nice guy. All

you're doing is letting her get under your skin and make you unhappy. And all she'll get out of it is more heartache when you finally do break it off. It isn't fair to either of you to string this thing along." Katie was never one to mince her words. She always called things like she saw it, even when it came to her own behavior.

Michael found that trait refreshing when it was just the two of them. When they were on the job, they both acknowledged it wasn't always a good thing.

"I'll take your advice under consideration. Have a good night." His comment was said gently, but effectively closed the topic to further debate.

Katie returned his smile and agreed to be picked up in the morning, then got out of the car and headed inside for a warm meal and a hot bath with a good book.

Later that night, Ryan Brewer popped into her head and she found herself wondering what he was like outside work. They didn't technically work together, so an attraction to him wouldn't be breaking her rules. She drifted off listing the reasons why it was a bad idea to develop a crush on Ryan, though she wasn't sure she was buying the excuses.

Four

After checking in at the office the next morning, Katie and Michael headed over to the medical examiner's office. Michael stopped at the coffee shop and got a non-fat caramel macchiato for Dr. Bennett. He knew she probably put in a late night, considering she was just starting an autopsy when he dropped off the records a little after six the evening before.

Stepping up to the glass partition that separated the autopsy suite from the viewing area, Michael tapped on the glass and held up the coffee cup for Dr. Bennett to see. A smile stretched across her face and she wrapped up what she was doing and stripped off her mask and gloves before washing her hands and exiting the room through the secure dressing area.

"You are a godsend this morning," she said as she took her first sip of the drink.

"You look exhausted, Marie. Did you get any sleep last night?" he asked. Michael had worked with Marie Bennett for years and was comfortable calling her by her first name. Katie didn't know her well and always reverted to her title, even though she had said to call her Marie.

"I made it home about two this morning, but I just couldn't rest knowing there were all these families needing answers. I came back in about seven and got started again."

Julie Mellon

As they talked, they walked down the hall to Marie's office. Once inside, they took seats on the comfortable couch and chairs to the left of her desk. The couch had made a comfortable bed for Marie several times in the past when she had worked late. Her husband had passed away ten years earlier of a massive heart attack and she'd never remarried. Once her children left for college, she became a workaholic and kept long hours.

"I've identified all our victims," Marie began with a swipe of her arm across her tired eyes. "The files you brought and the ones sent over by Brewer and Crawford were a huge help."

"Well, isn't that nice to hear?" Crawford's booming voice preceded him into the room, as did the smell of his cologne.

"What brings you here, Crawford?" Michael's tone turned cold. *Nothing could ruin a day faster than having to deal with this idiot,* he thought. Michael tried to keep his tone civilized, even if the one in his head was sarcastic, but just the sight of the man made his blood pressure rise.

"Well now, seems as if I'm the missing persons agent. If those bodies are my cases, seems I should be the first to know." Crawford swaggered over to the couch and sat much too close to Katie.

Katie thought of getting up and moving, but as she was the

only thing between Michael and Dane, she chose to stay put. At least she could try to block the punches should it come to blows.

"All right, gentlemen, I've had a long night and don't need the aggravation. Let's get down to business. First, I have renumbered the victims so they correspond to time of death. Now that we're comfortable that all the bodies have been recovered, I labeled the oldest remains as number one and so on, until we get to number thirteen, which has been confirmed to be Franklin Newberry."

"Oh, man. I'm sorry to hear that." The voice came from the doorway and everyone looked up to see Sheila Reynolds enter the room.

At the surprised look from Dr. Bennett, Katie quickly jumped in. "Marie, this is Sheila Reynolds. She's the missing persons detective from the Murfreesboro Police Department. I called her this morning and asked her to meet us here in case you had news."

"Welcome, Detective Reynolds. Come have a seat." Marie gestured to the last remaining chair. Once Sheila was settled, Marie continued with her identification.

"Victim number one has been identified as Daniel King. Number two is Lucas Bishop; number three is Patrick Harris.

These three were not particularly muscular and would have been relatively easy to overpower.

"Number four is Kelly Bishop, number five is Raymond Perkins and number six is Brian Ellis. These three were in very good shape. They showed signs of physical fitness and strong muscle attachment. Quite different from the first three.

"Number seven is James Darden. Number eight is Chad Montgomery, followed by Josh McDaniel, Miles Smith, Steven Edison, and Lyle Rhodes. None of these have any specific features of note. They seem to be moderately muscled. I haven't done full autopsies on them, just preliminary x-rays to compare dental records so you can do the notifications.

"Finally, we have Franklin Newberry. If he had been buried as thoroughly as the others, we wouldn't have the information I'm about to share. Hopefully it will help you in finding the killer. Mr. Newberry showed signs of being repeatedly tasered. There were twin imprints on his neck, lower back, buttocks, scrotum, and finally the bottom of his feet. I found other twin imprints on various parts of his body, but the decomposition to those areas was too much to definitively determine that he was tasered in that area as well. The cause of death is drowning."

Her final pronouncement was met with silence.

Finally finding her voice, Katie was the first to speak.

Free to Deceive

"Do you mean to tell me that someone put these men face-down in the water and tasered them so they couldn't raise their heads up?"

"I did some research last night after finishing Newberry's autopsy. Apparently repeated tasering can lead to many different scenarios. Muscle weakness is common after one use of a Taser. It takes up to several minutes to get your coordination back. Each repeated episode significantly delays the neurons from firing in the brain correctly. If there are too many repeated episodes, the person can go into cardiac arrest and die. I didn't see any evidence of cardiac arrest in Franklin Newberry so, yes, I believe he was tasered until he could no longer lift his head out of the water. And he was aware of what was happening the entire time."

No one in the room spoke for several long moments.

Dane was the first person to speak up, "Well, looks like we better get started making the notifications, Ryan. Let's start with the Newberrys."

"Like hell you will!" It was difficult to know who yelled it first, Michael or Sheila, but both were on their feet by the time the words were spoken.

"Now gentlemen --" Katie began as she stood. She didn't like being sandwiched between the two guys, especially as the only one sitting down.

Just as she got half way to her feet, Dane raised his arm intending to thrust it toward Michael but instead catching Katie on the side of the face. The smack echoed through the room forcing Katie sideways. She would have fallen if Michael hadn't caught her.

"What the hell is going on in here?!" The sound of Assistant Special Agent in Charge Nick Perry's voice rang out over the silence that had descended.

"I…um…I didn't…I'm sorry, Ms. Freeman," Dane stuttered.

"That's *Special Agent* Freeman, you arrogant, self-centered --"

"That's quite enough, Agent Powell. Why don't you and your partner go with Dr. Bennett and make sure nothing is broken. I'd like a word with Agents Crawford and Brewer."

As the three left, Sheila wisely ducked out along with them.

Once in the hall, Katie spoke up. "My face is fine, but that asshole's won't be the next time I see him."

"Let's get some ice on it anyway," Marie said and led the way back to toward the break room. She filled a towel with ice and handed it to Katie to put over her cheek, which was already red and swelling.

"You don't think he'll let them go before we have a chance to talk over the family notifications, do you?" Sheila tried taking the attention off Katie. She knew how difficult it was to be a female in this profession and knew that any injury would come across as a weakness.

"I don't think he'll see anything but the top of his desk and a whole lot of paperwork for the foreseeable future," Marie ventured. Though she hadn't said a word about Crawford, her demeanor had changed the minute he walked into her office.

"You don't like him much, do you?" Katie asked.

Marie just smiled. "I find it better to withhold verbalizing my opinions. I have to be neutral in order to do my job. I never start with preconceived notions and I never speak without concrete facts. I can only determine the outcome based on my own observations."

It was as close a confirmation of their assumptions as they were going to get.

Several minutes later, ASAC Perry joined them in the break room.

"Your face okay, Freeman?"

At Katie's affirmation, he continued, "Crawford and Brewer are going to continue on the remainder of the missing persons cases they brought forward with the hopes of identifying them among those recovered over the past few days. Since they're not among the victims, they're going to see if there is a connection between them. Those that have been identified have been reclassified from missing persons to homicide. The files are reassigned to Powell and Freeman. Please work with the local law enforcement units that have been handling the missing persons cases to coordinate notifications." With a nod to Sheila and Marie, ASAC Perry turned and strode from the room as quickly and quietly has he had appeared earlier.

Five

After Perry left, the four of them talked for a few more minutes. Even though it went unspoken, everyone knew it was really to give Katie time to keep the ice pack on her face. Before they left, Marie gave Katie ibuprofen and a bottle of water. Sheila, Michael and Katie drove to Murfreesboro and stopped at a Mexican restaurant just off the highway. The rain had finally stopped overnight and the temperature reached a sunny sixty-five. Sitting on the patio, they began making a timeline of the disappearances.

"According to Marie, Daniel King was the first body buried at the lake. He was reported missing in March of last year. So, in fifteen months, we have thirteen bodies. How is it that so many men could go missing in that timeframe and no one connected them?" Katie sorted the files by date of disappearance as she talked.

"We don't really have a good track record with interdepartmental or collegial collaboration. Some areas are better than others, but for the most part, we work independently. I did work with the Memphis department when Daniel King went missing because we weren't sure where he disappeared. What bothers me more is that there are only four of us on the MPD that work with missing persons and yet we have thirteen males connected to this area. I only knew about the two that were assigned to me until I received Newberry's case. We could've caught this sooner if we had communicated within our department."

Neither Michael nor Katie responded to that. She was right; a little communication could go a long way. But they both respected how she handled the cases that were assigned to her and that she took steps to make any connection between the two assigned to her and the disappearance of Franklin Newberry. That she showed the initiative to contact the FBI was a step in the right direction, especially if she intended to go further in law enforcement.

"I'm glad you made the connection between the three you were assigned. You have a very logical mind, which will come in handy for a police officer. Would you like to continue working on these cases?" Michael valued law officers who didn't carry an ego. With all the news lately concerning police brutality he felt a strong responsibility to mentor the younger officers who showed promise for turning around the reputation of law enforcement.

"I would love to keep working on these cases, but now that the bodies have been recovered, I don't see how that can happen." Sheila looked forlornly at the files containing her three missing persons. She wasn't ready to give up on these three men. After working for more than a year on the cases, she felt as if she owed it to them to find out what had happened. But missing cases that ended in murder were handed to homicide, or in this case, the FBI.

Katie picked up on where Michael was heading with his question. It was sometimes scary how they had managed to learn to read each other so well in such a short time. "We'll need a liaison with the local police, someone who's familiar with all these cases and can help coordinate the questioning of potential witnesses. It'll also help to have access to a local precinct to set up shop for the time it takes to make some progress on this case. Driving back and forth from Nashville between interviews doesn't make much sense and we can't keep using various restaurants."

As Katie talked, Sheila's eyes shone brighter and she was nearly squirming with excitement. She knew what they were offering was more than a liaison, but they had to frame it that way to get permission from her superiors. "I'm not familiar with all the cases, though."

"By the time we finish lunch and make the formal request you will be." Katie sat back in her seat so the waitress could place her fajitas in front of her.

Julie Mellon

While they ate, they rearranged the files several times. Beginning with the date of disappearance, then reshuffled based on sexual orientation. They identified three as gay -- one more than Sheila knew about -- one suspected homosexual, two confirmed straight and the rest were unidentified.

"I guess that shoots down my theory," Sheila said. She looked up from the paper she was using to take notes. Michael and Katie thought it would be beneficial to have the notes in her handwriting, to demonstrate to her boss how she connected the cases.

Next they sorted by age. Lyle Rhodes was the youngest at twenty, and Brain Ellis was the oldest at thirty-two. It was a larger age spread than they had expected, but made them pin the age of the perpetrator in the early-to-mid-twenties.

Third, they began sorting by physical description, but found that all the males were between 5'10" and 6'. All had brown hair with various eye colors. Their physical build varied from the muscular Brian Ellis to the scrawny Daniel King.

Finally, they attempted to put them in categories according to where they disappeared. Six of the thirteen had a connection to The Avenue: Franklin Newberry worked in a steakhouse, Josh McDaniel worked at a sporting goods store, Brian Ellis managed a gym in the shopping center, Patrick Harris worked at a

Free to Deceive

department store selling clothing, Lucas Bishop worked at a fast food joint, and Daniel King worked at a bookstore. Three members of this group -- Franklin, Josh and Patrick -- were known to be homosexual. Daniel King was thought to be, but they had no confirmation of that.

Chad Montgomery and Kelly Porter were from east Tennessee and there was no mention that they had traveled to the central part of the state. Kelly's twin, Kyle, stated in the missing persons file that he failed to show up for work at the zip line business they owned and ran together in the Smokey Mountains near Gatlinburg.

The remaining five had little information in the files, so assessing a place of disappearance was impossible. Michael noted that all five had been assigned to Zach Pryor, an MPD officer in Sheila's unit.

"What do you know about Zach Pryor?"

Sheila's face immediately puckered in disgust, as if just the mention of his name brought a bad taste to her mouth. "He's as arrogant as Dane Crawford. He could be Dane's father, actually - they're both cut from the same cloth. Zach is in his sixties, does as little as possible and wouldn't hand you a thimble of water if you were about to die of thirst; well, unless you were a good ol' boy. He has no use for women on the force and makes no bones about minorities knowing their place. He's a lawsuit waiting to happen. But the brass keeps him on a tight leash. He doesn't go out in the field anymore. I think they're just waiting for him to retire, which should be next year. Why?"

"Well, the five remaining bodies we recovered were all assigned to him and we have the bare minimum of information. Lyle Rhodes disappeared after school ended. There's no note regarding whether or not his belongings were found, or if they were still in his room. Steven Edison looks like he was written off as not returning to Tennessee. I don't even see a note on whether or not he followed up on if Edison made his flight back from Colorado. Miles Smith just has a note that he's a salesman. I don't even have a company name and I'm not clear on who reported him missing. James Darden missed a visit to the nursing home. Looks like Pryor just wrote "queer" on the file and left it at that. And finally Raymond Perkins didn't show up to teach his course at MTSU. Nothing further. There are no witness interviews or anything." Katie laid out the five files as she went over them. The information inside was all handwritten and brief. There were no timelines or printouts of credit card transactions. It's as if the five people had been reduced to a single sheet of paper with limited information.

Free to Deceive

Sheila shook her head. "Sadly, it doesn't surprise me. I try to look into as many of his cases as I can, but with a full load of my own, I can't always do it. Besides, he caught me doing it once and reamed me out good. Even went to our lieutenant. The problem is Lieutenant Watkins used to be Pryor's patrol partner, so he's protective of him. LT told me to watch my back, that Pryor could make life difficult and that I shouldn't make waves and just to wait out his retirement. Watkins is a good guy, but he doesn't stand his ground. Especially where Pryor is concerned."

"Will he give us a problem when we request to keep you as liaison?" Michael asked.

"No, not with thirteen bodies. I think he'll be more concerned that it not come out that some of these were never really investigated."

Michael nodded and they began packing away the files and paying their lunch tab.

Six

"Absolutely not! Reynolds is our newest detective in the department. If you need a liaison with MPD, we have senior officers who would be better suited." Lieutenant Watkins wasn't thrilled with the request from the FBI. He was adamant that someone more senior in rank than Sheila be assigned as liaison.

"Such as Pryor," Michael said sarcastically. He and Katie had been standing in Lieutenant Watkins office for over thirty minutes arguing over Detective Reynolds. Michael's normally pleasant demeanor was beginning to crack. All they had heard in the last half-hour was how inexperienced Detective Reynolds was and how there were other officers who could serve that purpose better.

If Michael was about to crack, Katie was already beyond irritated. She normally held her tongue and let Michael do the negotiations; not because he was a man or more experienced, but because she knew that he was better at finessing a situation. But now, they were beyond finesse and she decided to take over this situation so Michael didn't feel guilty later for being impolite.

"Lieutenant Watkins, there are thirteen bodies in our morgue, eleven of whom were originally assigned across your four detectives as missing persons. Detective Reynolds was the only one with the brainpower to connect the disappearances of these men. She recognized a pattern in these disappearances that may be what breaks this case. If you spent more time encouraging your detectives to work together and share information, these disappearances might have stopped before thirteen men had to die. We've been through all the files and seen the work that your detectives are capable of. Detective Reynolds is the only one who has demonstrated the ability to follow through on an investigation. She has done more than the basic background search on the cases assigned to her. The other files, and we have read them all, contain basic computer searches, if that. A missing persons case requires legwork and the only one around here who seems to be doing that is Detective Reynolds." Katie finished her speech with a pointed look at Watkins' distended belly, making it clear that she thought a little legwork would do him some good.

Complete silence descended on the room and the longer it stretched, the redder Lieutenant Watkins' face became. Neither Katie nor Michael backed down and if Michael thought Katie had overstepped a boundary, he never acknowledged it.

The face-off came to an end when Watkins stood up and strode to the door. Flinging it open, he bellowed, "Reynolds, get in here!"

Julie Mellon

Sheila walked in the office with her shoulders squared, trying hard not to show the smile that threatened to spread across her face at any moment. She knew Watkins was angry, but she also knew that most of it was for show. The only way he could keep the other detectives from rioting at this appointment was to show that he had no choice in the matter. Letting the others see that he was bullied into the decision by the almighty FBI was the only way for him to save face.

"These agents want you to work as their liaison for the next little while. Make sure your other cases don't suffer." Lieutenant Watkins resumed his seat and stared pointedly at the computer monitor until the other three left.

"I commandeered us a conference room for the foreseeable future," Sheila said. She began leading them down a pasty gray hallway, passed the desks of her coworkers and the break room. Entering the room, they noticed that she had begun affixing the photos of the missing men on the dry erase board at the head of the room. The first six were up and labeled, with the date of their disappearance, sexual orientation -- if known -- and place they were last seen clearly written underneath.

There was a female patrol officer in the room hanging the seventh picture. As she began to write the data beneath the photo Katie noticed that the handwriting matched that of the other six.

"Have you been doing this since I left you to guard?" Sheila asked the woman.

Jumping in fright, the woman turned around and faced the agents. "Sorry, I couldn't help myself. I know how hard you've been working on these disappearances." She ran a self-conscious hand over her black hair, which was pulled into a bun at the base of her skull. Of Latin descent, her black eyes shone with excitement to be doing something besides manning the front desk.

"Guys, this is my friend Gabriella Ochoa. She's been tossing around theories on these cases since I came up with the connection between the three. She's only been at MPD for three years, but is determined to make detective in the near future." As she talked, Sheila moved to the table and grabbed a dry-erase marker.

"How're we going to do this?" Sheila asked.

Gabriella resumed posting the information on the board while the other three took seats around the table.

"First, we need to notify the families that their loved ones have been found," Katie said. "For that, let's divide up the cases and do notifications in pairs. Sheila, why don't you and Michael go together? Since I don't know my way around and don't have a vehicle, I'm in need of a driver. Officer Ochoa, would you be willing to be my escort around town? This won't be a fun trip, but it will be a good learning experience for you."

Gabriella's eyes lit up at the prospect of being included on the investigation, even in a small way. "I'd love to!" Katie didn't have the heart to diminish her excitement by telling her that notifying family members that their loved one was dead was probably the most difficult part of any investigation.

"Okay, while you finish putting up the final photos and information, Michael will call the police departments in eastern Tennessee and have officers dispatched to notify their families there. Meanwhile let's divide up the cases for tomorrow so we can go through and conduct interviews after the families have had time to process their grief. We aren't in much of a hurry for information since these men have been missing for months. The forty-eight hour window is long closed. After we've completed the notifications, let's meet back here and regroup. Then we'll call it a night and resume in the morning. Does that work?"

Once everyone agreed, Michael began dividing the cases. Sheila wrote the appropriate name above the photo for the person who was going to conduct the interviews.

Michael's first assignment was to give the Newberry

interviews to Katie.

"But that's been my case from the beginning." Sheila said. She wasn't being argumentative; however, the protectiveness she felt over this case was apparent.

"We aren't taking you off the case. But you've talked to the family before and it might be helpful to have a new set of eyes and ears. When we reconvene to go over the interviews, you can compare what Katie heard with what you got out of them the first time. Sometimes a new person can ask a question in a different way and get different information. Also, having you free to interview the families of those that Pryor messed up will help tremendously. You have a gentle nature and knowing that the families will be upset about the lack of follow-through earlier means you're well suited for talking to them."

Michael's explanation soothed the worry from Sheila's face and she turned and wrote Katie's name above Franklin Newberry's photo. They continued on, assigning Katie to Newberry, Rhodes, McDaniel, and King. Michael was assigned to Edison, Smith, Darden and Ellis. Sheila was assigned to Perkins, Harris and Bishop. Montgomery and Porter were put on hold until they completed the first interviews in town and could schedule a trip to east Tennessee.

Gabriella tried to hide her disappointment as the

assignments were made, but everyone knew she wanted a role in the investigation. They all knew that having her involved would help her on her career track, too. Michael solved the problem with a few questions.

"What do you do, exactly, Gabriella?"

"Gabi, please call me Gabi. I mainly do background work. Pull records, check for outstanding warrants when traffic patrol pulls someone over, stuff like that. I've started helping homicide pull things like phone records and credit card statements."

A grin spread across Michael's face as she mentioned the last part of her duties. "How would you like to assist our computer gurus with pulling all the information on these thirteen men? They could show you the system they use to compile the information and search for patterns."

Gabi all but jumped up and down at that news. "That would be fantastic. I'm really good with computers. I'm sure I could keep up."

Getting her supervisor's name, the four of them left to begin the process of notifying the families before the news leaked to the press.

Seven

The scene outside MPD was a madhouse the next morning when Katie and Michael pulled up within seconds of each other. Not only were the local stations present, there were also two national news television broadcasters leading the charge toward the two agents as they approached the front of the building.

"Thank goodness we did the notifications last night. Remind me to ask if there's a back entrance we can use." Michael's normally laid-back personality was missing this morning. His brown eyes were red-rimmed and his hair looked like he had just rolled out of bed, but what gave away his mood more was the black shirt and tie he wore under a charcoal gray suit. In the months that she had known him, Katie had never seen him wear black.

Throwing out "no comment" as they walked in, Katie and Michael made their way to the conference room they had set up the night before. Andy and Lucy were already in the room setting up computers.

"Good morning," Lucy said in a deep, booming voice that was entirely too chipper for so early in the morning. "We can't devote all our time to you. We're in the middle of a case that's about to break wide open. When we heard you had a newbie down here, we got permission to conduct our ongoing investigation from here for a few days so we could monitor and mentor the kid. But just so you know, she'll be responsible for the bulk of the work on this case."

As usual, Lucy got straight to the point. She never stopped moving her large, six-foot frame as she spoke and by the time she was finished, three laptops were up and running. Her short-cropped red hair stood on end from where she continuously ran her fingers through it.

Sheila and Gabi came in a few minutes later and Michael performed the introductions.

"I hear you're good with computers. I always admire a woman who looks good with a…keyboard," Andy waggled his brows as he shook Gabi's hand. Andy had a quirky personality that often bordered on sexual harassment, though he usually knew where to draw the line. His colleagues at the FBI chalked up his inappropriate sense of humor to the fact that he spent his days tracking online sexual predators. He was the exact opposite of his flame-haired partner. Standing at barely five foot seven, his blonde hair was always immaculately combed and his hazel eyes held a lingering sadness from having seen too much darkness in the world.

Gabi laughed and returned the handshake. "I'm so excited to get started. Digging into people's lives this way is so much fun. It's like getting paid to put together a puzzle." She was practically bouncing on her toes as she spoke.

Lucy's booming laugh echoed in the room. "In that case, pay no attention to the stud muffin. I'm the true brains behind this operation." Lucy elbowed her partner aside so she could reach forward to shake Gabi's hand.

Leaving the tech geeks to begin their assignments, Sheila turned to the two agents. "Did you give a statement to the press already?"

"No, we gave the standard 'no comment.' I don't think we're ready to release anything yet. Why?" Katie was the only one standing in the conference room without a cup of coffee. She did, however, have her standard cup of sweet tea.

"They asked me about the connection between the bodies and the missing men from Murfreesboro. I heard a few names being tossed at me as I came in. Maybe one of the family members contacted the press."

Michael reached over and turned on the TV hanging on the conference room wall. The local morning news was running a segment about the bodies recovered in Smyrna over the past few days.

"…over the last year. While there has been no confirmation from investigators, several family members have confirmed that they were notified of their sons' deaths last evening. Among those were the family of Daniel King, James Darden, and Franklin Newberry."

The six investigators in the room looked at one another in astonishment. They hadn't told the individual family members the names of the other victims. The only way the reporters could have known about the names of the victims is if there was a leak from someone involved in the case. As they continued to listen, Katie became more and more angry over the thought of someone leaking information.

"It has to be Crawford. He's the only one arrogant enough to think he could get away with this. I bet this is his way of getting back at us for taking the case away from him." The longer she spoke, the angrier she became.

Michael quickly stepped in. "Well, the damage is done now. We need to contain the press. Let's put something together and go have a chat."

Thirty minutes later, Michael stepped up to the podium outside the Murfreesboro Police Headquarters, flanked by Katie and Sheila, and read the prepared statement.

"Yesterday morning, we identified the bodies of the thirteen victims that were recovered from Smyrna Park. We will provide you with the list of names at the conclusion of this briefing. The investigation into the deaths of these thirteen young men is ongoing. The FBI is working with all police departments involved in the missing persons cases, but will be based here in Murfreesboro and will be assisted by Detective Sheila Reynolds and Officer Gabriella Ochoa. We would like to thank you for your patience and understanding toward the grieving families as they are just learning of the unfortunate demise of their loved ones. At this time, we are not releasing any further information on this investigation. I'm willing to take a few questions, but there's not much we're ready to release."

As Michael finished his speech, the reporters began clamoring over one another to be heard.

"How did the men die?"

"Is this the work of a serial killer?"

"Is it true that all the men had brown hair? Do you think this is why they were targeted?"

"Did the men suffer before they died?"

"Should we alert the public to be watchful?"

"Do you have any suspects?"

Michael finally raised his hand to silence the group. "First, we have no suspects or persons of interest at this time.

Julie Mellon

The investigation is just now getting underway. We believe that all the men were killed by the same person. At this time, we are only prepared to say that it is always responsible to be watchful and alert to your surroundings. Yes, all the men had brown hair, but we do not know if that was a determining factor in why they were chosen. Eighty percent of the population has either black or brown hair. It's too early to say if this was the reason they were targeted. They have different eye colors and different builds, so going by hair color alone is a bit premature at this point. That is all for now. We will keep you updated with the most recent information."

The three turned and left the podium and returned to the conference room. Grabbing the files for their individual assignments, they each made their way to their vehicles and began the task of interviewing the family members of the deceased.

Eight

Knowing they had a better chance at solving the most recent murder, Katie opted to start her interviews with Franklin Newberry's mother. Making her way to the south side of the city, she pulled up in front of a single story ranch house that sat on a lot the size of a postage stamp. The yard was well tended with stargazer lilies that were starting to perk back up after all the rain. The green shutters stood out against the cream siding and the driveway was packed with cars.

Lifting her hand, Katie knocked on the front door, which was eventually opened by a middle-aged man whose skin looked gray. His bloodshot eyes took in her ID as she presented it to him and introduced herself. "May I have a few moments with Mrs. Newberry?"

The man opened the door further and invited her inside. "My wife and I just can't believe Frankie is gone. He's such a good boy."

They made their way into the living room where an overweight woman with mousy brown hair sat in the center of the sofa surrounded by other women.

"Honey, this is the FBI lady that came by last night, remember?" Turning back to Katie, he said, "She hasn't been herself since she heard the news. Do you know who did this to our boy?"

All the ladies in the room turned their eyes to Katie. Never one who was comfortable being the center of attention, Katie wished desperately that Michael were there. Squaring her shoulders, she shook her head. "I am so sorry for your loss. We're just beginning to get a handle on the situation. Is it possible to have a few words in private?" Katie didn't want to have this discussion in front of everyone.

For the first time, Mrs. Newberry spoke up. "These ladies are from our church. We have nothing to hide."

"Mrs. Newberry, this isn't about having something to hide, it's about protecting the facts of the investigation. There are some things that we are not ready to divulge but might come up in our conversation." Katie knew immediately that she had said the wrong thing when sparks began flying from the older woman's eyes.

"We have nothing to hide and there is nothing in your investigation that we will hide from our church. These people are our family."

Sighing, Katie decided to go ahead with the conversation, but to edit any details she might be asked about. If she revealed too much, there was no way to contain the information if one of these women decided to talk to the press. "Why don't

Free to Deceive

you start by telling me a little about Franklin? What was his everyday life like? Who did he hang out with? That kind of thing."

With quivering lips, Mrs. Newberry began talking. "Frankie was always a good boy. He sang in the choir at church until he enrolled in college and his schedule got too busy. He came by all the time to see us. We were so proud of him." As she realized that she would never again celebrate another of his achievements, she broke down in tears.

Her husband picked up the conversation. "He answered an ad his first year in college for a roommate. We didn't want him to leave here, told him he could stay as long as he was in school. But he was independent to the core. He moved in with that queer he's living with now. We didn't like it one bit - they're strange, you know. We told Frankie that he needed to be careful. Who knows what kind of diseases that guy brought in the house? Those people are'nt normal. Do you think that Sam guy had anything to do with this?"

When he started talking about Sam, all the church ladies looked up with stern expressions. Some covered their hearts with their hands, some shook their heads in disapproval, one even crossed herself, touching her fingertips to her forehead, chest and shoulder to shoulder -- not of Mr. Newberry's words, but of the thought that one of their own could have been corrupted by the 'evil gay' roommate.

"We've ruled out Sam as a suspect," she said. Katie kept her answer short. She wanted to say more on the subject, but knew she wouldn't get any further information if she smarted off about their opinions of homosexuals. Having been raised on a secluded ranch, Katie had never had formal religion in her life. But she couldn't help but think that if there were a God, he wouldn't want people to hate each other.

Mrs. Newberry sniffed and looked up. "Well, don't give up too quick on him. It wouldn't surprise me if it turned out to be Sam after all. He was always jealous of our Frankie. He even called him Franklin - as if Frankie would ever want to be called by his full name. *Hmpf!* Frankie always had girls flirting with him. He could have dated anyone he wanted to. He was just too busy trying to get his degree finished up. Once he became a teacher, he would have met someone special. Of course, even if he had time now, how could he do that when he had nowhere to take her? After all, what woman would want to be taken into a house with a man like Sam?"

Katie knew it was time to change the subject. Her temper wouldn't hold out much longer. "Tell me about his work."

"Oh, Frankie worked at the steakhouse from the time he was

sixteen. He started as a host, because he was too young to serve. But he loved being a server. He was promoted after he turned eighteen, even though they had to make accommodations because he couldn't serve the alcohol. See, we don't believe in drinking. But the manager at the restaurant was fine with someone else bringing the drinks out for him. Besides, he said all the lady servers were always extra nice and helpful. Our Frankie is a handsome boy."

Katie noticed the back and forth references to Franklin in present and past tense. His mother hadn't yet fully processed that he was never coming back home. She made a mental note to check about Franklin serving alcohol at work. "Can you tell me if there was a server who seemed more special to him?" Katie decided to play along with his parents' denials.

"Oh, he said there was one who flirted with him every time they worked together. He said she was nice enough, but not his type. My Frankie was never one to name names or to kiss and tell. He was very private that way."

The church ladies began telling Katie stories then, regaling her with all the great things Frankie had accomplished. Katie stayed a little longer and then wrapped up her questions and left to go meet with Daniel King's mother. From last victim to first. She could only hope Mrs. King was more understanding

Julie Mellon

of any choices her son had made.

Nine

Sheila was nervous as she drove to the offices of Raymond Perkins, Sr. He was a local attorney who liked to make mincemeat out of the prosecutors and witnesses at trial. Initially, she had been surprised to learn he was at work, but given his reputation, the surprise wore off quickly. She had never had any dealings with him, but Gabi had heard stories about the patrol cops who had to deal with him in court. She had decided to make this her first interview so that it wasn't hanging over her head, and also so that the other interviews could only look up from there. When you started at the bottom, there was nowhere to go but up.

Pulling into the parking lot behind a renovated century-old Victorian home, she stepped out of the car, smoothed her hair down and adjusted her jacket over her sidearm. Entering the lobby, she was greeted by two smiling receptionists behind a large, mahogany desk that stood at chest height.

"Welcome to Perkins, Ingram, and Greenbaugh. How may I help you?"

It took all of Sheila's willpower not to laugh when she realized that the firm initials would be P.I.G. It summed up her opinion of the profession perfectly. "I need to see Mr. Perkins, please."

Julie Mellon

"Do you have an appointment?" the blonde-haired, blue-eyed, pre-pubescent looking receptionist smiled as she asked.

"Not exactly, but when I called earlier, he said nine o'clock would be a good time to stop by."

"I'm sorry, but without an appointment, I'm afraid Mr. Perkins doesn't have an opening."

Sheila let her temper get the better of her. Leaning forward with her elbows on the counter she looked the receptionist directly in the eyes and enunciated each word carefully. "My name is Detective Sheila Reynolds and I am here to talk to Mr. Perkins about the murder of his son. Now pick up the damn phone and let him know I am here."

The little girl's eyes grew to the size of saucers as she quickly picked up the phone and whispered into it. Seconds later, she hung up and ushered Sheila through the door into a conference room with a table large enough to seat twelve. Placing two bottles of water on the table, she turned and left just as Ray Perkins Sr. walked into the room.

"Thank you, Amanda," he said. Closing the door behind his receptionist, Sheila couldn't help but notice the appreciative glance he gave as he watched her sashay away. "Thank you for coming to my office, Detective. How can I help you?"

Shocked at his question, she said the first thing that

popped into her head. "You are aware that your son was murdered, are you not?"

With a resigned sigh, he sank down into the chair at the head of the table and ran a hand across his tired eyes. "Yes, Detective, I am aware that my son was murdered. He's been missing since August. When you do what I do for a living, the only logical scenario is that he's dead. I have known since I reported him missing that he would never return. I may sound callous, but I have had nearly a year to come to terms with that fact. I'm glad that he's been found and that we can lay him to rest. It'll do his mother some good to do so. I fear that despite my trying to prepare her for this eventuality, she held out hope that he would come home some day."

Sheila regretted her tone and the question. Taking a sip of her water, she took a deep breath and tried to repair the impression she made. The more information she could get from him, the better the chances of solving this case.

"Can you tell me why it took you a week to report your son missing?"

Chuckling, he answered, "My son was a very private person. He always said any conversation with me was like getting the third degree -- said he always felt like he was being cross-examined. He started keeping secrets in his teens and as soon as he turned eighteen he moved out. He went to Vanderbilt, got his Bachelors in history and followed that with a Masters degree. He was enrolled in the Ph.D. program and taught at MTSU for extra income. I provided him with a place to live, tuition and such, but he refused any more assistance than that. His first class was on a Thursday and when he didn't show up, we just assumed he had gotten his weeks mixed up. The schedule for MTSU was different than Vanderbilt, which didn't start until the following week. We didn't think much about it. But when he didn't show up on Tuesday, we knew something was wrong.

"He had mentioned something about going on vacation with a girl he was seeing. While I thought he was being honest about the trip, I didn't believe for a minute it was with a girl. I know my son. Even if he never admitted it, I know he was gay. Some things a parent just knows. Anyway, I checked his credit cards, but there was no trace of any purchase of airfare or hotel rooms. He just disappeared one day. It still bothers me that I don't even know what day that was."

"Mr. Perkins, we've started to believe that this might be a hate crime. That perhaps this was someone targeting gay men. One of the things on my list to find out was whether or not your son was gay. You say you know he was, but do you have any proof, or do you know who he might have been dating?"

Free to Deceive

Shaking his head before she even finished the question, Mr. Perkins responded, "I only have my suspicions. But it isn't normal for a teenage boy and then young man to never talk about girls. He was always a guy's guy. Even in high school, he only took friends to the dances. He never stayed out past curfew or snuck out of the house. When he watched television, he never gushed over the women on the screen. He just wasn't your typical horny teenager. And he never would have mentioned the name of someone he was dating. Like I said when this started, he was a very private person and his mother and I respected that. We wanted what was best for him and tried to let him know that we would always be there for him."

Sheila asked a few follow up questions, but there was nothing more to learn. Expressing her condolences one last time, she left the building to head to her interview with Lucas Bishop's sister.

Ten

Michael pulled out of the Murfreesboro police department and headed toward Gayle Darden's home. He was relieved that this was his first interview -- at least he didn't have to navigate the waters of asking a loved one if they knew or thought the victim could be gay. His compassionate nature had already suffered having to deliver the news of their deaths. He didn't want to now compound their loss by asking potentially sensitive questions.

James Darden had been co-owner of a gay nightclub that operated at the edge of The Avenue shopping center. It was an unusual location, as all the businesses around it closed up by nine; just about the time The Open Closet got into full swing. It was common for some of the club's patrons to stop and have dinner or do some shopping before coming in for an evening of drinking and dancing.

Taking a seat in the comfortable living room, Michael couldn't help but notice the abundance of photos in the room. Jimmy was one of five children and there wasn't a surface or wall in the room that lacked a photo of the various siblings at some embarrassing stage of development.

"Can I get you something to drink?" Gayle Darden asked, wringing her hands in front of her. She was a nervous little

Free to Deceive

woman, barely standing five feet tall. If ever there were a holdout from the 1960s, this woman was it. Her paisley top and bell-bottom jeans clashed with the floral print on the sofa. There was a rotary dial phone on the table beside the chair and crocheted doilies covered every surface -- they even draped over the back of the couch cushions.

"A glass of water would be nice," Michael replied. He knew giving her a task would help her relax.

Once he had his water and Gayle sat in the chair, Michael cleared his throat. "I'm very sorry for your loss, ma'am. Are you up to telling me a little about your son?"

"Oh, Jimmy. He was a darling boy. He was born smiling and reaching for the nearest dress. His sisters loved to dress him up and parade him around the neighborhood. From the time he was two I knew he was gay. I made sure he knew he was loved just the way he was. You know, most parents don't do that. It's why the government is able to twist their minds. If parents taught their children better, then schools wouldn't be able to warp their minds." She stood up and gathered the glasses they had been drinking from and took them out of the room, even though Michael hadn't touched his.

Michael took a second before replying. The wide-eyed expression on Gayle's face made him wonder if she had been medicated. As he had the thought, a younger version of Gayle - dressed in modern clothing - walked into the room.

"Hi, I'm Ginger, Jimmy's sister. My mother is something of a conspiracy theorist. She thought the government had Jimmy locked away these past few months. She thought they were doing experiments on him and that he would be home at any time." Shaking her head, her reddish-blond hair swayed back and forth down her back.

Gayle reappeared in the room with a stack of papers. She had apparently overheard her daughter's comments. "Well, since that wasn't the case, you should look at his business partner, Nathan Dixon. He was embezzling from their business."

"Now, mother, let's not start on that again."

"Don't you 'now, mother' me. I know what I'm talking about. Here." She thrust a stack of papers toward Michael. "You just take a look at those. My Jimmy knew something was going on. He brought those over here a week before he disappeared -- asked me to hold on to them for him. When he didn't come back, I read them. There are all kinds of receipts in there -- notes and such. He didn't trust Nathan, but I don't fully understand what all of it means."

Michael flipped through the papers, but couldn't make heads or tails of what they were supposed to contain

Free to Deceive

"Do you mind if I keep these?" he asked.

Gayle shot him an exasperated look. "I wouldn't have given them to you if I didn't intend for you to use them as evidence. You just write me a receipt showing you're taking them."

Doing as she asked, Michael wrote a receipt on a piece of paper from the spiral notebook she produced. After a few parting remarks, he left the house to go talk to Nathan Dixon.

Eleven

Lindsay Bishop owned a small boutique specializing in handmade items that was tucked in the corner of The Avenue. The woman running the cash register waved Sheila to the back room where she found Lindsay unpacking boxes of new merchandise. Her eyes were red and swollen and tears continued to flow down her cheeks. Sheila cleared her throat to announce her presence and watched as Lindsay wiped away the tears before looking up to greet her.

"You all finally decided my brother's disappearance was worth investigating, huh? Now that he's dead?" The bitterness in her tone was unmistakable, as was the pain in her eyes.

Sheila silently cursed Zach Pryor for his shoddy police work and for putting her in the position of having to apologize for him. She really wanted to ring his neck and then drag him by the balls to face every family of a missing person that he failed to investigate fully. But she was unable to say that to this woman without opening the police force up to a lawsuit; besides, it wouldn't change the outcome of why she was there. Biting her tongue on these thoughts, she brought her mind back to the purpose at hand.

"I'm so sorry for your loss. This must be a difficult time for you and your family." Sheila easily kept her tone

Free to Deceive

compassionate. She truly felt for Lindsay and all those who lost family members to violent crime.

"I don't have family anymore. It was just Luc and I. Our mom died a few years ago and our dad hasn't been around since we were small. It was always just the three of us -- as far back as I can remember. It was hard when mom died, but at least I had him. I'm not sure what I'll do now." As she talked, the tears began streaming down her face again. She didn't bother to hide them or try to stop them. She just swiped an impatient hand across her cheeks as if she had cried enough and they were an annoyance.

"Can you tell me what happened to him? I didn't get much information last night. Did he suffer?"

Did he suffer… Sheila hated that question. Normally she could lie about it, but since this case was big and getting bigger, she knew that if she told a falsehood now it would come back to bite her later.

"Keep in mind we are not releasing details of the case to the media. It makes it easier to apprehend the person who did this if some of the facts are kept out of the public arena. I can tell you that your brother drowned in the pond where he was found. Judging by the condition of his body, we believe that it was near the time of his disappearance. That means he wasn't kept hidden somewhere for any length of time." She watched as Lindsay winced at the thought of her brother drowning, and then as the relief that it wasn't a prolonged death crossed her face.

"Can you tell me more about the day he went missing?"

Sitting down on the top of a box that had yet to be opened, Lindsay motioned for Sheila to pull up a separate box to sit upon. "His roommate called me that morning. Rob and Luc have been friends since they were in diapers. They did everything together. They had gone shopping the afternoon before, but parted ways after that. They had a fraternity dance that night. When Luc didn't come home that evening, Rob figured he was just running late. But when Luc didn't show up at the dance and was'nt in their room by the next morning, he called me. We started looking around and found his car in the parking lot at The Avenue. His cell phone was there with a text that hadn't gone through. He tried to text Rob to tell him to come to the store. No one had heard from him since."

"Can you tell me where in the parking lot you found his car?" Up until now, there hadn't been a clear connection between any of the other victims and The Avenue.

"Sure. It was beside the tuxedo and dress shop. There was a spring formal for Lucas and Rob's fraternity and they had picked up vests to match their dates' dresses."

"Oh, was Lucas dating anyone?"

Lindsay chuckled. "No, no one serious. He liked to keep his options open. I always teased him about not getting serious with a girl, but he said he didn't need anyone serious because he had me." A sad smile played across her lips as she finished speaking.

"I don't mean this to be insensitive, but do you think it's possible that Lucas might have been gay?" Sheila held her breath as she asked the question but Lindsay just burst out laughing.

Pulling herself together and wiping a different kind of tears from her face, she shook her head. "There is no way he was gay. Our uncle who took us in after mom died was gay. We talked about it a lot. He definitely liked women, too much so sometimes."

Sheila thanked Lindsay for her time and left her to finish her inventory with a promise to keep her updated on the progress made in the investigation.

Twelve

Pulling into the parking lot of The Open Closet, Michael took a few minutes to sort through the papers he received from Jimmy Darden's mother. There was a spreadsheet printout showing dates, deposits, and cash register totals. Handwritten notes were added, but the handwriting was nearly illegible. Attached to the printout were cash register tapes and copies of deposit slips. Even without the notes, Michael could see that approximately twenty percent of each night's income was never deposited. He put the paperwork in the glovebox for later and decided to get a feel for Dixon knowing he would bring Katie back later to get the benefit of her intuition.

Getting out of the car, he made is way into the dimly lit bar through the back door.

"We're closed. The doors will open for business tonight at nine."

The man who spoke stood about five foot ten with thinning hair. He wore jeans and a polo shirt and was standing behind the bar taking inventory of the bottles lining the mirrored shelves. There was a large raised wooden area on the opposite wall that served as a stage for the drag shows that were popular on certain Thursday nights. A staircase to the right led up to the dance floor above.

Free to Deceive

"I'm here to see Nathan Dixon. Know where I can find him?"

With a huff, the man turned around. "I'm Nathan. Guess you must be that FBI guy who called me earlier. Can I offer you a drink?" He motioned to the bottles behind him despite it only being ten-thirty in the morning.

Michael shook his head and reached out to shake hands. "This is a pretty nice place you have here. How's business?"

"I can't complain. Jimmy was a mastermind when it came to ideas for the bar and how to bring in customers. All I had to do was keep track of the money and the bills. We were turning a nice profit. I don't come in during business hours… not really my scene if you catch my drift. But I hear that the place is packed every night we're open."

Something about his answer bugged Michael, but he couldn't figure out what it was. Nathan gave too much information for such a simple question. He seemed nervous. Perhaps it was just because he was talking to the FBI. Those three letters had that impact on some people.

"What are you planning to do now that Jimmy isn't around to run the day-to-day stuff?"

"Well, as soon as a death certificate is issued, I'm planning on selling the place. I think it's time to move on, start a new adventure. Any idea how long that will take?"

Julie Mellon

"Well, the medical examiner has thirteen bodies to autopsy. Going in order of their recovery, Jimmy appears to be seventh on the list. It's going to take several weeks at best." This news wasn't what Nathan wanted to hear.

"Damn it!" Slamming his fist onto the bar top, Nathan shook with what appeared to Michael as a combination of fear and exasperation.

"It's bad enough that his airheaded mother has been refusing to sell his portion of the business to me for the past seven months. I mean, come on. It's only common sense that if someone disappears for this long he isn't planning on coming back. But no, she keeps insisting her 'little Jimmy' will be back any day. The woman is a nut. She actually thinks that the government gives pregnant women certain drugs so that the fetuses are pre-determined to follow a certain path. She thinks DNA is a code word for this drug, not the genetic make up of our bodies. For real, the woman is bat shit crazy. And she has kept me in limbo for seven months. I was nice enough to wait a month after Jimmy disappeared before talking to her about selling the place. But noooo. She wouldn't hear of it. 'This was my Jimmy's dream.' That's all she kept saying. She even started interviewing for a club manager to take over until Jimmy comes back - as if she doesn't trust me to run my own damn club."

Free to Deceive

Considering the proof he had in the car, Michael thought it was no wonder the woman didn't trust him. Not ready to tip his hand to this knowledge, Michael asked a different question instead. "What can you tell me about Jimmy's everyday life? His mother said he dated around, but didn't get serious with anyone."

"Yeah, that's true. He was still too busy sowing his oats. He loved women's clothing -- he was very popular on the stage. He went by the name Gemma when he was performing. Off the stage, he liked to be the life of the party, didn't matter if he was Jimmy or Gemma. The employees and customers alike loved him. In fact, his dressing room hasn't been touched since he disappeared. The other performers have practically made it a shrine to his memory. There are bags in the room full of clothes he purchased just before he disappeared -- he hadn't even gotten to take the tags off yet."

Michael thought it was interesting that Nathan knew so much about how the customers interacted with Jimmy when he claimed that he never came during business hours. He was definitely looking forward to introducing Katie to him.

"You mind if I look around, maybe take a look in that dressing room?"

"Not at all. Just go through the door to the left of the

stage. You can't miss it." It was obvious Nathan hadn't spent much time around the theatre or stage, otherwise would have referred to the door as 'stage right.'

Making his way slowly across the bar and through the door Nathan indicated, Michael took a long perusing look around the place, trying to get a feel for it. Once in the back hallway, he made his way to the last door on the left, which had a plaque on the outside that read 'Gemma.' The bags Nathan mentioned were sitting on a leather couch -- the label on the bags were from a department store in the same shopping center. Inside, there were several sequined tops as well as a leather mini-skirt.

To the right of the door was a dressing table that held the typical mirror with lights ringed around the edge. There was enough make-up on the tabletop to stock a cosmetics counter. Overall, the room was impeccably neat but yielded nothing obvious that would lead Michael in the direction of his killer.

Returning to the main room, Michael left his card with Nathan and walked back out to his truck. On the way, he ran into Sheila, who was wrapping up her interview with Lucas Bishop's sister. Deciding to grab lunch, they called Katie to have her join them.

Thirteen

Daniel King's mother lived six blocks east of the Newberrys, but there was a world of difference in the neighborhoods. Where the Newberrys' house was standard middle-class, the Kings lived like, well -- kings. The large colonial house sat back from the street with a manicured lawn and neatly trimmed hedges. The driveway arched up toward the house and ended at a three-car garage that opened on the side. From the driveway, Katie could see a large in-ground pool with a pool house behind it.

Walking up to the door, she rang the bell and heard it echo through the rooms beyond. The woman who answered the door was dressed in pressed pants and had her hair pulled back into a French twist. The only signs that she was grieving were the reddened and puffy eyes that looked out at Katie. Once again showing her identification, Katie asked to come in.

Introducing herself as Regina, the woman ushered Katie into a formal sitting room and offered her a drink. Knowing that the woman needed something to do with her hands, she accepted a glass of iced tea.

"Mrs. King--"

"Oh, please call me Regina. I haven't been Mrs. King since my husband left me for his secretary ten years ago."

Julie Mellon

Katie smiled slightly and nodded. "Regina, can you tell me about Daniel? What was his everyday life like? Who did he hang out with? That kind of thing." She began with the same questions she had asked the Newberrys.

"Daniel… that sounds so formal. We called him Danny when he was small, but as he grew up, he preferred Dan. Daniel was his father's name and they never got along. Daniel was very domineering and exacting. He wanted everyone and everything to be perfect. Dan could never measure up." Shaking her head to get her mind back on track, Regina took a small sip of her tea.

"Dan was always shy and quiet. He was small for his age his whole life. When he was a kid he used to get picked on and bullied. Of course, back then we didn't call it bullying. It was just kids being kids. But it hurt his feelings deeply. He might have taken it better if he didn't have to come home and face it here, too. We tried putting him in sports but he just never had the ability and the teasing was worse when he couldn't perform on the field. When he was in high school, he learned to play chess and found he was really good at it. He had such an intellectual mind. He was always very studious, so it didn't surprise me when he started working at the bookstore. It was the perfect job for him. He received his degree from MTSU in literature. He talked a lot about becoming a writer. He had such an imagination." A small, sad smile briefly appeared on her face.

"I'm sure none of this is what you need to know. I just don't know what to tell you. I can't imagine anyone wanting to hurt Dan."

Katie took a drink of her tea as she thought over how to approach the next subject. "Regina, can you tell me if Dan was dating anyone?" Playing it safe, she left out any reference to his possibly being gay.

"Oh, not currently. He started dating a girl in high school -- they were sixteen -- but her family moved away right after graduation. Susie stayed here in town and went to MTSU. They lived in a small apartment their first two years, but started growing apart. They decided to take a little breathing room and got their own places for the last two years of school. They broke things off last year, just before he disappeared. She was a sweet thing -- just as shy and awkward as he was."

Katie made note of the break-up, wondering if they had really grown apart, or if Dan discovered he had other interests. She needed to ask the question gently. "We've tentatively come across a theory for these deaths. Do you think it's possible that Dan was gay?" She was careful not to use the word murder, but couldn't come up with another way to ask the question. For the second time today she wished Michael were with her.

Regina chuckled. "Oh, I thought that many times. But he was always interested in girls. Of course, he was too shy to talk to any of them. However, he was small, so if that's an assumption that has come up in your investigation, then I suppose it was possible that someone could've assumed he was gay. You should talk to Jack Patterson. Lately, he was Dan's closest friend. At Dan's age, I am sure there are things he wouldn't talk to me about."

Nodding, Katie made note of the comment. "Just one more question. Did you or your son know Franklin Newberry? They live about six blocks from here." It had occurred to her on the drive over that even if they went to different schools, they might have played together at the park that was located halfway between their homes.

"Not to my knowledge. The name doesn't sound familiar. Of course, he didn't have many friends and didn't socialize much."

Drinking the last of her tea, Katie wrapped things up with a few more remarks and headed out.

As she stepped on the porch, her phone rang. Answering, she said, "Hey, Michael, what's up?"

"Sheila and I are meeting at the steakhouse for lunch. Can you join us? We can go over what we've learned so far."

Free to Deceive

"Sure, I can be there in fifteen minutes." Hanging up, she got in her car and began the drive to The Avenue.

Fourteen

Arriving at the table just as a tall, stout waitress was taking Michael and Sheila's drink order. The waitresses face still had a childish look to it, though she appeared to be in her mid-twenties. Katie smiled as she approached and watched the waitress tuck her thin, lank hair behind her ear while looking Michael up and down. Jutting one hip out to the side and propping her hand on the table, the waitress asked, "Are you sure that's all I can get for you, sugar?"

Uncomfortable, Michael adjusted his tie and caught sight of Katie standing behind the waitress. "Katie, what would you like to drink?" He quickly diverted attention from himself causing the waitress to spin and look at the newcomer.

The waitress, whose nametag read Susanne, gave Katie a once over and dismissed her. Turning back to the table, she repeated the two drinks already ordered. "So that is a water and a Dr. Pepper."

Katie felt her temper rise. She wasn't good with interpersonal skills in an ideal situation, but add in irritation and she had a tendency to be snarky. "Actually, that would be a water, a *coke* and a sweet tea. Thank you." She squeezed between Susanne and the table, causing the other woman to step to the side, and sat down in the booth beside Michael.

Free to Deceive

When the waitress didn't move away, Katie looked up expectantly.

Susanne gave an indignant huff and left the table.

"You better hope she doesn't spit in your tea," Michael chuckled. He was used to Katie's reaction to people. When he first met her, he thought her reaction was simply because she didn't care what people thought. But as he learned more about her, he came to realize it was more a matter of her upbringing and her ability to read people.

She was raised on a secluded ranch that seemed like a prison. Although she never revealed specifics about the place, he knew that her mother restricted her access to the outside world. She had learned to read people by observing the women that came to live on the ranch. Only being allowed to observe, she never learned the skills to respond. Now, she was one of the best partners he had ever worked with when it came to immediately sensing whether a person was being honest or if they had something to hide. As long as he took the lead when needing to finesse a situation, they had a great system that had led to a quick closure on their first case together. He hoped this one would be the same. There were so many people involved that he didn't like her not having first-hand access to all the interviews. But unless they wanted to take six months to talk to everyone, it was necessary to spread the interviews among the three of them.

Katie wrinkled her nose at Michael. "She wouldn't dare. Besides, I can see the drink station from here. I'm keeping an eye on her."

They made small talk as Susanne returned with their drinks - sitting Michael's down last with an extra-toothy smile for him. She took their orders and shot a nasty look at Katie before leaving.

Sheila and Katie snickered once she walked away.

Alone at last, Katie got right down to business. "Sheila, why don't you start us off? Anything interesting?"

"I might have busted our theory. Ray Perkins, Sr. is pretty adamant that his son was gay. I thought it might be validation that my idea was on target. But Lindsay Bishop says there is no way her brother was gay." She seemed discouraged by the setback, but there was still an underlying determination in her eyes.

"Don't be so quick to discount yourself. You added one more to the list of gay men. Do we have a picture of Lucas Bishop? It might be possible that someone looked at him and used stereotypes to reinforce an opinion that he was gay -- whether or not it was true. Let's keep that thought in mind as we get more information on the other vics," Michael reassured Sheila. In an investigation you never ruled out any theories until there was definite proof that it wasn't a possibility.

"I talked to Jimmy Darden's mother and sister," Michael said. "The mother was nuttier than a fruit cake, but might have a valid theory. It bears looking into, though I don't know how it would apply to the other men." He outlined the conversation he had with Nathan Dixon and handed the papers Gayle Darden had given him to Sheila.

"We should see if any of the other victims had a connection to either The Open Door or Dixon," Michael stated. "Regardless, we should get someone to look into the business records. Sheila, why don't you pass this paperwork on to Gabi and have her look into it?" As he finished speaking, Susanne arrived with their food and they were forced to pause until she wandered off again.

Katie dug into her soup before taking her turn in reviewing her morning interviews. "I started the morning with the Newberrys and crew. They had a house full of church friends that they felt had a right to know everything. I didn't want to reveal too much of our theories to them, so I didn't mention anything about Franklin being homosexual. They were vocal enough about it without me bringing it up. They even went so far as to blame Sam Blackstone for Franklin's death. Overall, not much to learn from the interview. I got the feeling that Franklin went to great lengths to hide his life from his family.

"I had a more interesting conversation with Daniel King's mother. It actually relates to something you just said, Michael. His mother said he dated a girl from the time he was sixteen until he was twenty-two. They lived together the first two years of college but things started falling apart. They broke up a few weeks before he disappeared. She said he wasn't gay, but was small in stature and his manners might be interpreted as effeminate. I definitely think we should look into Lucas Bishop's mannerisms to see if there might be room for misinterpretation."

"Can I interest you in dessert?"

Katie looked up to see Susanne standing at the edge of the table. Though her eyes were focused only on Michael, there was something in her posture that made Katie think she had heard part of the conversation. She was a large-boned woman who didn't wear make-up and Katie wondered if she might be offended at the thought that people use physical appearance as a means to determine sexual preference. Given the woman's overt advances toward Michael, Katie had a feeling that Susanne might have been on the receiving end of such an assumption.

They all refused dessert and asked for their checks just as Sheila's phone rang.

"It's Gabi. Let me see if she has something for us. I know

she was going to look into everyone's backgrounds starting this morning."

"Hey, Gabi, what's up?"

While Sheila was on the phone, they each handed over their payment to Susanne and waited through all the "uh huhs" and "ohs" until finally, Sheila ended the call.

Gabi was so excited that the phone practically vibrated in her hand as she dialed Sheila's number. She debated on whom she should call, finally deciding on Sheila only because Gabi wanted to make sure they were kept in the loop. There had been a lot of talk around the precinct about how the FBI would come in and take over, leaving everyone else out of the loop. Gabi didn't get that sense from Katie and Michael, but wanted to make sure -- at least until she got to know them better.

"Hey, Gabi, what's up?" Sheila's smooth voice came through the line.

"I might've found something that can help. I thought I would make a few easy inquiries to get used to the system Andy and Lucy are showing me. First, I checked out Steven Edison and he did make his flight back from Colorado. I'm checking to see if I can track his movements once he landed back in Nashville. I'll get back to you on that.

"Second, I looked at the manifests from the flights that Brian Ellis's girlfriend said he was on. According to his missing persons file, his girlfriend reported him missing when he failed to return from a body-building competition in Miami. There's no record of him on a flight to Miami; however, there is a flight to Orlando and a four-night cruise in his name. He was accompanied by Keri Eldridge -- on the flights and the cruise." As she finished rushing through all she had discovered, she finally stopped to take a breath and waited for what seemed like forever before Sheila replied.

"Sorry, I was giving the waitress my payment. That's good information. We'll talk about it and see what we think. I hope it comes to something."

"That's it?" The disappointment was obvious in Gabi's tone.

Sheila chuckled. "It's good work, Gabi. And it puts us one step closer to something. Keep looking and lobbing things at us to check out. I bet some of the information you uncover will break this case wide open. But I can't tell you that just by hearing the information. We have to investigate it. I promise, you'll be the first to know if something you discover turns out to be the key."

"Okay. I guess I have to be happy about that. Staring at this computer is a thankless job." Gabi tried to keep the dejection in her voice from coming through the phone. She was determined to double her efforts and find the one crumb that would lead to the whole cookie.

Hanging up, Sheila relayed what she learned.

"Interesting," Michael said. "I had the girlfriend on my list for this afternoon. I'll try to squeeze in both women."

They spent a few more minutes coordinating their afternoon interviews before agreeing to meet back at MPD for take out and updates.

Fifteen

Katie found Jack Patterson patrolling the lot of the used car dealership where he worked. He was an attractive and fit guy, but the cheap suit and fake smile gave him a smarmy vibe.

"What can I do for you, Agent?" He flashed his megawatt smile when he saw Katie's badge.

"I'd like to talk to you about Dan King." Katie was immediately repulsed by Jack's attitude. She felt like she needed a shower to remove the slime he was directing her way.

"Ah, I heard he was found. Tough break for the kid. He had it hard enough without this added to his troubles." There was no sympathy in Jack's tone. He could have just as well been talking about the features of the nearest vehicle.

Swallowing her knee-jerk desire to be sarcastic in favor of getting more information, she remarked, "His mother says you were his closest friend at the time he disappeared. Can you tell me what was going on in his life?"

Jack looked uncomfortable for a moment. "Well, I went into the bookstore about three months or so before he disappeared. He was sitting in the cafe area reading a book about understanding your sexuality. When he tried to hide the cover from anyone looking his way, I made a joke about it. He turned five shades of red and stammered, trying to find something to say. I told him he shouldn't be embarrassed by who he was and that's how our friendship started."

There was something about the way Jack wouldn't make eye contact and kept shuffling his feet on the ground that raised Katie's suspicions.

"Are you gay, Mr. Patterson?"

The megawatt smile reappeared on his face. "Well now, I like to think of myself as equal opportunity. Pretty lady such as yourself would catch my eye just as quickly as a nice looking fellow like Dan. Attraction comes in all forms and I say we should embrace it as it comes."

Katie was all for accepting people as they are, but this guy was slick and sleazy. "Did you date Dan King?"

"We went out on several dates. Hung out a lot. He had a hard time coming to terms with his father. Boy had severe daddy issues. I spent months trying to get him to talk to his mom, or at least to accept who he was. About a week before he disappeared, we got together. It only happened once and then he vanished. When he didn't answer my calls or show up to work for a few days, I figured he couldn't handle what happened and backed off. It wasn't until the police detective came by that I knew he had been reported missing. He was shy and depressed and didn't know where his life was headed, but that man loved his mama. If she couldn't find him, I knew something had happened to him. It's a shame that he ended up like that."

When Jack said it this time, Katie could see a small trace of remorse hidden in his eyes, but it was quickly replaced with the mask he wore to hide who he really was.

"One more thing. I assume you've seen the news with the release of the other victims' names. Do you know any of them? We're looking for a connection between any of them."

"Are you insinuating I had something to do with this?"

Katie knew immediately she had said the wrong thing. Damn, why wasn't Michael with her today?

"I'm not insinuating anything, Mr. Patterson. I just thought that maybe some of them had come here and bought a car, or that you might have seen them when you were at The Avenue. You mentioned you met Dan in the bookstore, so you shopped there. It's possible you might have observed some of them there." She thought she did a good job of backpedaling and held her breath to see if Jack would respond.

Huffing out a breath, Jack let his chest deflate and the indignation leave his posture. "I know Jimmy, the owner of The Open Closet. I go there a lot. Lucas Bishop and Lyle Rhodes came there too. The others didn't look familiar."

Thanking him for his time, she headed back to her vehicle

Free to Deceive

as Jack turned his salesman smile at another customer. Katie heard the woman giggle at Jack's greeting and rolled her eyes as she got into her car.

Sixteen

Before dropping the paperwork from Michael back at the precinct for Gabi, Sheila headed toward the home Patrick Harris had shared with his boyfriend, Brad Collins. They lived in the end unit of a string of townhomes near The Avenue.

The man who opened the door made Sheila take a second look. "You're Robbie Ellwood, right? You were at Sam's house when we came to talk to him about Franklin?"

Robbie smiled. "Yes, that was me. I brought Franklin over to visit with Brad when we heard that Patrick was found as well. We all used to hang out together and it's nice to have the support system with two of our circle gone."

As he talked, he led Sheila into the dining room where Sam sat at a table with another man who looked as distraught as he did. A third man was sitting there and was introduced as Edward Harris, Patrick's brother. When Robbie took a seat next to Edward and took his hand, Sheila guessed from the interaction that the two were a couple.

"I'm sorry for the loss of your friends and I don't mean to intrude, but we're trying to get a jumpstart on this investigation. It would be really helpful if I could ask a few questions."

Edward was the one who spoke up and his tone was anything

but friendly. "Where were you when we reported Patrick missing? You didn't seem to care then."

Brad reached over and took his other hand. He turned his head to Sheila and the bleakness in his eyes nearly brought her to tears. All she saw in her mind was that one word written in Patrick's missing persons file. *Queer.* As if that explained everything and summed up the worth of his life. Never before had she had a stronger urge to kick Zach Pryor's ass for not investigating his cases properly than she did right now.

"You're right. We screwed up. I wish I had been assigned to Patrick's case from the beginning. It might have saved a lot of lives. I was assigned Dan King's case when he disappeared but the next missing male I was assigned was Josh McDaniel, six months later. It wasn't until I received Franklin's case that I saw a connection. That's no excuse, but I do want you to know that I'm truly sorry for your losses." Sheila was careful to make eye contact with all four men sitting around the table. She knew her words were meaningless -- they wouldn't bring Patrick or Franklin back. But she wanted them to know that their deaths wouldn't be ignored any longer.

With a sigh, Brad wilted in his chair. "What do you want to know?"

"Well, I was going to start by asking if you knew any of

the other victims. With all of you here, maybe you can brainstorm and connect a few dots for us. I don't know if Sam shared our theory with you or not. We're exploring the possibility that this might be a hate crime; that someone targeted these men because they were gay. We've since found out that some of the victims were not gay, but their mannerisms might have been interpreted as such."

Brad actually chuckled at that statement. When he saw Sheila's confused look, he explained. "Patrick was the most non-gay gay man I have ever met. We used to joke that if he weren't coming home to me every night I would never know he was gay. He had a normal build, not scrawny, but he didn't really work out. He had a fast metabolism and could eat anything he wanted and stay skinny as a beanpole. Some people have all the luck." Realizing what he had said, Brad dropped his face into his hands. Edward reached over and reassuringly patted his back.

Sheila pulled the fliers that contained the missing persons information, including pictures of the known victims. These were the fliers that had been printed at the time each man had been reported missing and had been circulated in the community. She handed them to Brad who laid them out on the table one-by-one.

"This first guy, Dan, he worked at the bookstore. I knew him to say hello, but didn't even know his name. He was shy, but never really paid any attention to anyone. He always kept his head down. Patrick used to say he wanted to inject him with some courage. We called him the little lion -- like he hadn't grown up enough to realize he needed to find his courage."

Flipping to the second one, it was Sam who recognized him. "This guy frequents The Open Closet." Sheila made a note as Brad flipped the third paper over and saw Patrick in the photo.

The four men took a minute of silence as they looked at the flier until Brad reluctantly flipped the fourth one over.

No one recognized Kelly Porter, which didn't really come as a surprise as he was one of the two victims from out of town. She had been hoping that one of them *would* recognize him -- at least it would have provided some kind of link.

They flipped through the rest of the fliers, only recognizing Brian Ellis from the gym, Jimmy and Lyle from the club, and Franklin.

Sheila asked a few more questions but didn't learn anything more than that Edward and Patrick had been disowned by their family when they came out. Edward had admitted being gay after Patrick, more as a form of solidarity than from a need to admit the truth. He didn't like how his parents reacted and knew he would rather live as who he was with the support of his brother than live a lie with the ridicule of his parents. They had one other brother who lived in Portland. He still talked to them regardless of the family's wishes. He was married with two small children, so they didn't talk often, but he was accepting of them both.

Sheila left the townhouse and headed to the precinct to turn over the paper from Dan's mother for Gabi to begin investigating.

Seventeen

Michael groaned with dread when he first saw Melissa Smith. She was tall, thin, blonde, and dressed from top to bottom in spandex. To be fair, she was just completing a run, but wearing only a sports bra and tiny little spandex shorts was a bit too much of a cry for attention to be exercising just for the health benefits. She reminded him too much of his girlfriend, Candice, and it immediately put him in a bad mood. Pushing his unhappiness with his current dating situation aside, Michael climbed out of the car and approached her house as she stepped up onto the porch and began stretching.

"Excuse me," Michael said, at eye level with her nicely toned backside as she bent over and placed her palms flat on the concrete below her.

Instead of straightening up and turning around, she twisted sideways and peeked at him from around her kneecap. Michael watched as her eyes swept up and down his body. Apparently liking what she saw, she licked her lips and wiggled her hips a bit.

"What can I do for you, handsome?"

Michael flipped open his identification. "Special Agent Michael Powell. I'd like to talk to you for a few minutes about Brian Ellis."

Julie Mellon

A sour look crossed Melissa's face as she stood to her full height and raised her arms over her head to stretch.

"I haven't talked to that lecherous man since Labor Day last year. Why do you want to talk to me about him?"

"You haven't seen the news today, ma'am?"

Pushing out her bottom lip into what he figured she considered a seductive pout, she replied, "You don't have to call me ma'am. My name's Missy."

He nearly laughed. Missy was as ridiculous as Candice wanting to be called Candy. He just couldn't do it. There was a time in a person's life that they needed to be grown up and calling a woman in her late twenties or early thirties 'Candy' pushed the limits of his patience. Again shaking off thoughts of his girlfriend, he forced himself to smile politely at *Missy*. He couldn't control the sarcasm of his inner voice.

"I'm sorry to be the one to tell you this, but Brian's body was recovered yesterday. We're looking into his death and since you were dating him at the time of his disappearance, I need to ask you a few questions." Michael wasn't sure exactly which day Brian's body had been uncovered, but he figured that detail wasn't relevant in the scheme of things.

"Wait a minute, he really did disappear? I thought that was just an excuse for him to break up with me without having to do it to my face. What happened to him?" Her shock appeared genuine, but Michael was just thankful that her flirtatiousness had disappeared.

"His body was found in Smyrna along with the bodies of twelve other men over the past several days. From what we can tell, his body was buried around the same time he disappeared." Though Dr. Bennett hadn't confirmed this, it was an assumption he was comfortable making due to her comment about the various stages of decomposition and the fact that it appeared Franklin Newberry had been buried around the time he disappeared. He made a note to bring this up during the debriefing that night.

Missy sank down on the top step of the porch and took a long drink from her water bottle. "He was a two-timing scumbag, but he didn't deserve to die." Her blue eyes filled with tears that overflowed down her cheeks.

"How long did you date? What makes you think there was another woman?"

"We were together for about eight months. I wanted something more serious, you know? Something more than a one-date-a-week relationship. I swear the only reason he even bothered taking me out was so he could sleep with me. I guess he figured as long as he wined and dined me I wouldn't mind putting out. But I loved him and I wanted more. He said he wanted to continue having an open relationship. It doesn't take a genius to figure out from that comment that he was seeing other people. He left to go to a bodybuilding competition in Miami and said we would talk when he got back. But he never came to get me when he returned from the trip. I just thought, good riddance to bad rubbish. Wow, I can't believe he's really gone."

"Missy, can I ask you something that might sound ridiculous?"

At her nod, he continued. "Do you think it's possible that Brian was gay?"

Missy burst out laughing and water sprayed from her mouth. Coughing to clear some water that she inhaled, she finally broke out into giggles.

"That is the most hilarious thing I have ever heard. There is no way he was gay. He was 100% male." She was breathless from laughing and coughing.

Michael didn't bother to correct her by informing her that gay men were 100% male as well. He understood the gist of her comment, even if it was phrased in a derogatory manner.

He talked to her a few minutes more, but when she became more interested in trying to get his number than in answering his questions, he hastily wrapped things up. *Next time, I will sic Katie on her. She won't know what hit her.*

Free to Deceive

Michael smiled at his thoughts as he plugged Keri Eldridge's address into his GPS.

Keri could have served as Missy's twin -- tall, fit, blonde hair, blue eyes. The only difference was that she was dressed in business attire, having just returned home from a day at the office.

She was less than thrilled when Michael asked to talk to her about Brian Ellis. "I only have a few minutes. I'm due at the gym in half an hour." She was brisk and didn't look pleased to be talking about him.

"How did you meet Brian?"

"At the gym. He was my personal trainer for a while. We were both single, or so I thought. I was flattered when he took an interest in me. We had been dating for about two months when he asked me to go to the Bahamas with him. I needed a vacation, so I went. That man was insatiable in bed. But when we got back to Florida to catch a plane home, I saw a text message on his phone from another woman. He was surprised that I thought we were exclusive. After he stopped calling me, I discovered there were at least six other women he was seeing. I stopped going to the gym for a while, but a friend said he no longer worked there, so I went back."

"How did you find out he was missing?"

"I didn't hear he was missing until around Christmas. A group of us were in spin class and the instructor was gossiping with another gym employee. I overheard their conversation. I have to say, I was surprised when he left the gym. He loved it there. There were ready-made dates, women who liked having their ego pumped up which made them more willing to sleep with him."

Michael asked a few more questions, but she made it clear that she knew nothing more and needed to go. Bidding her a good evening, he headed to a Chinese place near the precinct and got a variety of take-out dishes to bring to the debriefing meeting.

Eighteen

When Katie got to the precinct, Michael was already there with Gabi and the smell of Chinese food made her stomach growl. Michael was leaning over Gabi's shoulder as she excitedly explained something on the screen.

"Great job, Gabi," Michael encouraged. "You're really catching on to this system."

The thud of her heart hitting her stomach surprised Katie. She quickly dismissed it as possessiveness of her partner. She didn't like Michael working with anyone else -- surely that was it. *It doesn't matter what I like. He's my partner, so he's off limits. Besides, you're already lying to him.* Pushing down the guilt, she turned to the food and began looking at the options. The other two had already begun eating.

"Where're Andy and Lucy? Sounds like they've been good teachers." Katie thought she did a good job keeping her tone neutral as she spooned fried rice onto a plate and topped it with a chicken and mixed vegetable dish. Michael's raised eyebrow made her doubt that she was successful.

Oblivious to the interplay between the two, Gabi piped up. "They left a few hours ago. Something about a task force meeting for the case they're working on. They couldn't say much, but their case sounds fascinating."

"There isn't anything fascinating about child predators." Katie's tone was harsher than she meant and the shocked look on Gabi's face, as well as the frown on Michael's, immediately made her feel guilty. The fact that she caught on to the cues was a sign that she was improving in her social awkwardness. She also knew that her reaction was unfair and had nothing to do with Gabi. She was really going to have to work harder to clamp down on this attraction to her partner.

"Sorry, Gabi. You didn't deserve that. I'm just cranky because we haven't caught a break in this case. Out of thirteen victims, we can't even figure out a common thread."

Michael gave a small smile of approval at her apology. "We'll get there. It's only been one full day since we started turning over stones. Gabi has a few things to share regarding Nathan Dixon. As soon as Sheila gets here, we'll get started."

"Did I hear my name, and is that food for me?" Sheila came in and plopped her bag on the table, immediately grabbing a plate and starting to load it with food.

"Lunch seems so long ago. I need to put some snacks in my purse."

The room was quiet for several minutes as everyone ate enough to take the edge off their hunger. Gabi was the first to finish her plate of food.

"I have a bit of information about Nathan Dixon. Why don't I start while y'all finish eating?" At the nods from around the table, Gabi went to the dry erase board at the front of the room and outlined what she found.

"Nathan is a gambler. He's in big with some serious loan sharks out of Nashville. He's tried to borrow money from several banks, both personal and business loans. The personal loans were denied based on his credit, which is abysmal. The business loans required Jimmy Darden's signature. I don't know if Nathan asked him to sign and he refused, or if Nathan decided it wasn't worth asking, but none of those loans were approved.

"Secondly, Nathan has been lining up potential buyers for the club since about six months before Jimmy disappeared. I talked to a few of the buyers on the phone and they all stated that Jimmy refused to sell. Apparently, owning this nightclub was his dream. He wanted to buy out Nathan's share but couldn't get a loan on his own. Apparently the banks wanted a solid five-year history of a successful business plan. They were one year short when Jimmy disappeared.

"Third, and I think most interesting, Nathan was under investigation by our narcotics squad." Gabi moved to the table and handed out folders to the other three before resuming.

"There has been an investigation going on at the club for

the past eight months -- a few months after Jimmy disappeared -- regarding the sale of recreational drugs. They're close to connecting the operation to Nathan, but he's careful to remain hands off and in the background. From what they say, he's becoming more desperate for money and is starting to get sloppy."

"Great job, Gabi." Sheila praised her work while Katie and Michael nodded in approval.

"This fits in with what I was thinking." Katie stood and moved to the board to peruse the information that had been added.

"I think we've been pigeonholing this investigation." Noting the crestfallen look that Sheila was trying to disguise, Katie made an attempt to be gentle. "I'm not saying that the angle we've been pursuing so far is wrong, just that we latched onto it without considering other options. That's a fatal mistake in a lot of cases. Sheila handed us a great theory that might end up being the solution. But being part of a team means bouncing around ideas. We haven't done that. From the beginning we split up and took off in four different directions trying to prove one theory. We need to let the evidence speak to us."

Sheila took a deep breath. "Ok, you said this fits with what you've been thinking. Is there anything specific or just that we haven't explored all the options?"

"Mostly that we just haven't looked at any other direction this case could be going. When Michael showed us those papers at lunch, it really made me realized how narrow-minded we've been. Then I talked to Jack Patterson and had another thought. He just seemed slick to me. And he claims he was dating Dan before he disappeared. I think there is more to him than what he said. I also asked him about the other men and if he knew them. He got angry but did admit to knowing a few from the club. Maybe the connection is more than The Avenue, maybe it's The Open Closet? But then that takes us right back to our theory of a hate crime."

Sheila went through her interview next. "Sam Blackstone and Robbie Elwood were with Brad Collins when I got there. When I saw all of them together, I had the same thought Katie did; maybe there was a bigger connection. I had them look through all the fliers of the victims to see if they knew any of them. It was pretty much the same as Jack Patterson -- they knew Franklin, Patrick, Lyle, Lucas, and Dan. They all agreed that they could have met the others, but just weren't sure enough to say yes."

Turning the floor over to Michael, the women laughed at the grimace on his face. "While you all were conducting serious interviews, I got stuck with the Barbie Twins. Brian Ellis definitely had a type. Melissa -- or Missy as she likes to be called -- seemed more interested in getting my number than answering questions. She didn't show any particular sadness for his death other than a few tears, but she was definitely bitter about their break-up. Keri was very matter-of-fact. She stopped going to the gym after their break-up, but eventually rejoined when she learned he no longer worked there. Apparently the gossip took a few months to reach her."

They spent a few more minutes asking questions of each other and getting general impressions of the people they interviewed before dividing up the assignments for the morning. Agreeing to meet at the precinct at noon to have lunch, Katie was assigned to talk to Josh McDaniel's co-worker and Lyle Rhodes's roommate. Sheila would go along with her. Michael was going to talk to Miles Smith's boss and Steven Edison's girlfriend. Gabi was tasked with looking more into Jack Patterson. They all agreed to review what had been learned so far for ideas on new theories to lay out at their lunch meeting the following day.

Katie agreed to pick Sheila up at the precinct at eight, effectively ending a long day's work that had yielded little or no results.

Nineteen

Pulling up to the precinct on Thursday morning, Katie got out of the car and headed toward the conference room. She brought along three large drinks she picked up from a nearby coffee shop. She had a caramel macchiato for Andy and a double shot hazelnut latte for Lucy -- their favorites. She had observed Gabi loading her coffee the previous day with all the fruit flavored syrups in the station, so she opted to get her a white chocolate raspberry latte.

Walking through the hoard of reporters, Katie tried to ignore the questions being thrown her way, but she stopped dead in her tracks as one question penetrated her hearing.

"Agent Freeman, we have a source close to the investigation saying that you are investigating this as a hate crime. Is that true? Is that why the FBI was called in?"

Katie looked up and around, and the reporters quieted down as they seemed to catch on that one of their questions had struck a chord with the normally recalcitrant agent.

"The FBI was called in because the bodies of thirteen men were found in a mass grave. We have not narrowed our theories to any one in particular yet. This case is ongoing and any source that claims to be 'close to the investigation' is feeding you false information. There are four people on this case and I can guarantee that any information you have didn't come from any of us. Once we have more information, we will pass along what we can. Excuse me." Katie resumed walking, having to push between several of the reporters who were not happy with the limited information she gave.

In the hall outside the conference room they had commandeered for the task force, Katie ran into an older detective, his gold shield clipped to the waistband that was barely visible for the overhang of his stomach. The door was open and Katie could see Lucy and Andy talking with Gabi. Their conversation wasn't audible from where she stood, but apparently it was from where the detective was standing.

"Can I help you?" Katie didn't like the attitude coming off this detective. He carried himself like a schoolyard bully and was scowling at the occupants of the room.

"Well, well. If it isn't the little eff bee eye lady." He sneered as he took a step in her direction, keeping his voice low enough so that it didn't carry into the room.

"Special Agent Katie Freeman, and you are?" She kept her tone casual and extended her hand in greeting.

"I'm Zach Pryor. I was just looking in on a case that should've been mine. I'm the senior missing persons detective.

Guess it just goes to show the favoritism we gotta show to the ladies nowadays. Give 'em what they want, keep 'em happy. As long as it ain't between the sheets. You ladies shoulda stayed in the bedroom and outta the boardroom. We were better off without you around here. They let you in here and now all of a sudden it takes a task force to solve the case of a missing queer. Hell, they go missing all the time. Usually shacked up with the meat-of-the-month. Another abomination, you ask me. Just wait 'em out. They'll show back up."

It took every ounce of willpower Katie possessed not to take this guy down. She was fit enough and skilled enough to do it. Instead, she raised her voice so that it carried into the conference room and around the corner to where the other missing persons detectives were sitting, including their commander.

"Detective Pryor, I'm appalled by your attitude. It's exactly your lack of tact and concern for these victims that allowed thirteen of them to be murdered before any connection was made. As I'm sure you've heard by now, these men were not 'shacked up with the meat-of-the-month' as you so eloquently phrased it, they were murdered. Waiting them out didn't work in this case, now did it? *They were murdered* and no amount of waiting would result in them turning up." Katie wanted to say more to drive home the point that these men were killed because of his attitude. But nothing she said would get through all his prejudices.

"Is there a problem here?" Lieutenant Watkins rounded the corner and took in the sight of his detective staring down an FBI agent -- his hands on his hips and his face beet red. Agent Freeman stood tall, her back ramrod straight, fists clenched around the drink carrier containing the coffee. It took all her power to squelch the urge to toss the drinks in his face. She was the one to speak.

"Your detective here thinks that these 'queers' just need time to finish up their recent love-fest. That there's no need to investigate what happened. Oh, and he also thinks us female investigators are just hysterical and stirring up trouble where there is none."

Pryor just snorted, but he did step back and lower his arms.

"Detective Pryor, whey don't you return to your desk? I'd like a word with Agent Freeman." Lieutenant Watkins waited until Pryor was out of hearing range.

"You'll have to pardon him. He's been the senior detective for years and as I tried to tell you and your partner the first day, appointing the newest detective to this case was bound to start trouble."

Free to Deceive

Katie couldn't believe what she was hearing. Despite Sheila telling them that Watkins and Pryor had a long history, she thought for sure he would recognize the importance of this case.

"If you were more interested in getting results and answers on the cases that come through your department instead of playing nanny to cry-baby detectives, thirteen men wouldn't be dead. I don't need to overlook him. He needs to be taught to get along with others. If his attitude toward others is impairing his ability to do this job then perhaps it's time to remove him from active cases. You aren't doing anyone any favors by catering to his bad attitude."

Stepping around the lieutenant, Katie entered a conference room to find four pairs of eyes focused on her. Placing the coffee down on the table, Katie turned to Sheila.

"Perhaps we should get out of here before he yanks you off this case."

Sheila's eyes widened, but she hurriedly grabbed her purse and the two of them made a beeline for the door.

Twenty

The morning passed quickly and Michael, Katie and Sheila gathered in the conference room. Katie made sure to firmly close the door this time.

Andy, Lucy and Gabi looked up as the door clicked into place. As they all gathered around, Katie started the discussion.

"First, there are two things I need to mention. This morning I had an exchange with Pryor and Watkins." She gave them a rundown of what had transpired and how she had lost her temper. "I have a feeling we'll need to be quick and thorough on this or Watkins will try to pull Sheila and Gabi."

Thinking Michael would be disappointed in her for the exchange, Katie was surprised when he chuckled.

"I'm glad you stood up to them. They certainly wouldn't have listened if I had been the one to say anything. If they try to pull these two off, I'll talk to ASAC Perry. I hear he's close friends with the MPD Chief. I wouldn't worry too much. In fact, I might just call him anyway and let him know the situation. At least then he won't be blindsided. What else?"

Relief coursed through Katie at the support from her partner, which made it even harder to keep her guilt at bay. Her last partner in Louisiana had been quick to take the credit, but even faster to place the blame. Her two years there had been miserable.

"Second is that someone is leaking information." The others in the room began protesting. Katie held up her hand.

"I know it isn't anyone in this room, but the first thing I was asked this morning by the reporters outside was if we were investigating this as a hate crime. They cited a 'source close to the investigation.' My money is on Pryor being our leak. We need to plug it. From now on, our conversations are behind closed doors. When Michael, Sheila and I aren't here, you three need to keep the door closed." The last comment was directed at Gabi, Lucy and Andy. They nodded their agreement, each of their faces reflecting their distaste for this betrayal.

"Did you address the question with the media?" Michael spoke up.

"I did. I told them that we were in the beginning stages and just now conducting interviews, that we weren't limiting ourselves to just one theory. That was all I said, because I didn't want to say anything that would let them know we have nothing."

As she finished speaking, a knock sounded on the door. Andy opened it to find a pizza delivery for them. Putting the pizzas on the table, they all dug in and began reviewing the morning.

Julie Mellon

After grabbing a few slices, Michael recapped his morning. "Well, I started off with an eight-thirty meeting with Donnell Harmon. He runs the security firm where Miles Smith worked. There wasn't much to learn. Miles had appointments all day, but failed to return that evening with the equipment he used for demonstration purposes. The company rule is that all equipment be locked away in inventory every night. When he didn't show up to turn it in, Harmon called him. When he got no answer, he called the police. They traced his cell phone to the parking lot of The Avenue, beside the steakhouse. Donnell started calling the customers he was supposed to meet that day and found he only made the appointments before lunch. The last appointment he showed up to was with a client at the steakhouse. From there, he vanished.

"Next, I went to interview Darlene Hise, girlfriend of Steven Edison. She works retail at the bakery in The Avenue shopping center. He left to go to Colorado for a bachelor party/ wedding of one of his college frat brothers. She was supposed to go, but at the last minute, the bakery received an order for a large wedding. She says they talked several times while he was gone and that he called her as he was boarding the plane to come home. They agreed to have dinner at the steakhouse once he returned, but he never showed up. She reported him missing once the first twenty-four hours passed."

Michael's shoulders slumped as he finished. He hadn't discovered anything that could be a smoking gun.

Gabi piped in, "I verified that Steven Edison did, in fact, make the flight back to Tennessee. His vehicle was found in the parking lot outside the bakery the next morning. His cell phone and car keys were found inside."

Katie nodded to Sheila to indicate that she could recap their interviews.

"We started with Derrick Winston, Josh McDaniel's co-worker at the sporting goods store. It turns out that they were actually dating. They kept it quiet at work, but weren't secretive about it. Their families were tolerant of their relationship, though they lived out-of-state. Derrick said they were both scheduled to work that day. His shift started at one and Josh was supposed to show up at three. They were scheduled to close the store and had made plans to go from there to The Open Closet for a while. Josh never showed up. Derrick tried to call him, but there was no answer. Once his shift was over, he went home to see if maybe Josh was sick, but no one was there. He returned to The Avenue, thinking maybe Josh had his schedule mixed up. He found his car in the lot, phone and keys inside. He called the police and Detective Pryor took over."

Julie Mellon

Taking over their report, Katie outlined their next interview. "Andy Cross was dating Lyle Rhodes. They met at The Open Closet a year before Lyle disappeared. They moved into an apartment together before the start of the school year. Both were scheduled to take exams the week Lyle disappeared and had scheduled a study session. Lyle never showed up, but Andy didn't worry until a classmate in his exam asked why Lyle had missed the exam earlier that morning. When he returned to their apartment, there was a message from Lyle's mom asking why he hadn't made it home for a scheduled visit. Apparently he made it a point to visit his mother after each semester so she could pamper him with his favorite foods. She had everything ready, but he never arrived.

"Andy called Lyle's mother and found he still wasn't there, so he started retracing his steps. He started by calling the sandwich shop, where he learned that Lyle had clocked out the previous evening when the store closed at eleven. When workers showed up that morning, Lyle's car was still in the lot. They didn't think anything about it, figuring maybe he had been picked up. His cell phone and keys were inside."

Sheila took over to recount their third interview.

"The story is pretty much the same for Lucas Bishop. We took his sister's advice and talked to Rob Callis, Lucas's

Free to Deceive

roommate. In this case, they were actually just roommates. Both were heterosexual. They spent the morning of his disappearance shopping for tuxedos for a fraternity formal. Rob said everything was fine. Lucas was his normal self, he flirted with a few women in the department store -- the same one Patrick Harris worked at -- they had lunch at the fast food place where he worked. They parted ways after that. When Lucas failed to show up at the formal and then his date showed up to ask why he didn't pick her up, Rob knew something was wrong. He called around, but got no answer. Lucas was known for not getting serious, but no one thought he was the type of guy who would stand a girl up. They decided to enjoy the dance. The next morning, when Rob still couldn't find Lucas, he called Lindsay. Later that day, his car was found in The Avenue parking lot, phone and keys inside."

Twenty-One

"There are a lot of similarities here." Leave it to Andy to state the obvious. Everyone shot him a look that conveyed the 'well, duh' sentiment without saying a word.

"Hey, don't shoot the messenger. It's not my fault that none of these connections were made. If the MPD had entered even one iota of this information into the crime system, this connection would have been caught. Only three of these thirteen disappearances were logged in, and all three of those were Sheila's."

Sheila blushed at the praise, even though it was earned. Gabi beamed at her friend and gave her two thumbs up.

Standing and walking to a second dry erase board she had requested Gabi find, Katie took a marker and wrote 'NEW THEORIES' across the top.

"Let's start by making a few connections," she said.

She added a column to the board for Gay, Straight, and Unknown. Gabi started a spreadsheet to track what was written. With assistance from the rest of the group, they began filling in the information. Under the Gay column they wrote: Dan, Patrick, Jimmy, Josh, Lyle and Franklin. Six of thirteen men fell into that category. Under the Straight column, they wrote:

Free to Deceive

Lucas, Ray, Brian, and Steven. Listed as Unknown, were Kelly Porter and Chad Montgomery from Knoxville and Miles Smith.

"Okay, let's move on from there. I was thinking last night about my interview with Jack Patterson. What if this isn't a crime of hate, but a crime of passion? Maybe Jack or someone else was rebuffed by these guys. They all, with the exception of the Knoxville guys, seem to be involved in relationships. What if a guy came onto them and was upset to be rejected?"

"I like it," Michael spoke up, "but why does it have to be a guy? Why not a woman?"

Seeing the confused looks directed his way, he continued. "I interviewed Missy Smith and she was very bitter about Brian's deception. She's tall and fit. She could easily overpower some of these guys. Since we know from Franklin Newberry's autopsy that there's evidence of repeated stun gun use, we can assume that it would also be easy for her to overpower the three fit guys -- Porter, Perkins and Ellis."

Lucy stood up from the table; at her full height she was six feet tall. She was a very large-boned woman and carried her extra padding well. Her spiky red hair stood out in all directions. Waving at Michael, she said, "Lay down on the ground."

Michael looked at her with his mouth open. "Excuse me?"

"I'm physically fit, strong, and tall. I might not be the beauty that Missy and Keri are, but I can at least help you test your theory." Lucy used her famous self-deprecating wit as she spoke.

Doing as she asked, Michael pushed a few chairs aside and lay down on the floor.

"I've always wanted to put my hands on you," Lucy cooed as she knelt down beside him. Katie thought, *me too*, but kept her comment inside -- then berated herself for having it in the first place.

Instructing him to lay still and be dead weight, Lucy grabbed his arm and pulled his upper body into a sitting position. Lowering her shoulder, she managed to get his rib cage up and over then wrapped her arms around his waist and lifted with her legs. A lot of grunting, sweating and cursing later, she managed to get to her knees where she juggled Michael's body to move him forward more until he was hanging across her shoulder in a fireman's carry. Slowly, she stood to her feet and turned to deposit him on the top of the conference table.

"Dessert is served, ladies." She smiled as she backed away quickly before Michael could sit up. "Are either of the Barbie Twins as big as me?"

Michael shook his head as he resumed his seat and

Free to Deceive

straightened his magenta tie.

Andy spoke up next. "Maybe two of them worked together? If he was seeing that many, it's possible they decided to get revenge as a pair. Maybe they decided to continue to punish any guys they thought were cheating. Didn't you say Lucas was flirting with several women while he and his roommate were shopping? What if he flirted with the wrong woman?"

Sheila and Katie exchanged looks.

"Why do I get the feeing I'm going to be back on the ground again?" Michael said dryly. He got up and lay back down on the carpet.

Katie moved around the table so she was at his feet while Sheila grabbed under his shoulders. On a count of three, they heaved him upward. It took several tries, but eventually they were able to hoist him onto the tabletop, bumping his head into the arm of a chair and his hip into the edge of the table.

As he landed with a thud, they all heard someone clear their throat from the doorway.

Looking up from her position between Michael's legs, Katie came face-to-face with her boss, ASAC Perry.

"Well, this looks interesting. Is this how we solve cases now?"

Michael calmly swung his legs off the table, got to his

feet, and once again straightened his tie. "Hello, sir. We were just testing a theory."

"And that would be…?"

Lucy snickered but quickly covered it with a cough.

Katie couldn't look at ASAC Perry -- her face was so red it was nearly purple.

Michael just barked a laugh. "We were wondering if it was possible for a woman to be responsible. You missed Lucy trying to lift me from the floor on her own. She did it, though. But none of the women we've interviewed so far match her physique. So we wondered if two women could be working together. Detective Reynolds and Agent Freeman are both fit, so they gave it a shot. Since I'm roughly the weight of the biggest of the men, I was the lucky one who got to play dead."

"Well, glad to see you've come back to life." He smirked before turning a frown toward Katie. "I hear you've been stirring the pot with the locals."

Ready for a dressing down, Katie straightened her spine and finally looked ASAC Perry in the eyes. "That man is a bigot. And his boss is an ass. I held my tongue as long as I could. But when he told me that women were better off staying in the bedroom and out of the boardroom, I had enough. Then he had the audacity to go on and state that the lives of 'queers' weren't worth the trouble we were going through to investigate. It wasn't my intention to stir up trouble, but the situation called for it."

They all waited in silence, barely breathing, waiting to hear the outcome of this morning's argument with the locals.

"I'm glad you stood up to him. Chief Snyder received a complaint, which he brought to me. He's been aware of this situation for a while now and just needed an excuse to push the issue. When it was just internal, no one here would speak up -- the blue wall and all. He crossed the line when he shot his mouth off to someone outside the MPD. I just wanted to let you know that you're all still on this investigation -- but make it quick. We don't need anymore bodies. If the timing holds true, you only have until next week before this person strikes again."

Once the door closed behind ASAC Perry, they all stared at each other. Finally, Gabi broke the silence.

"I can't believe we missed that connection." She stood up and moved to the board containing the data on all the victims. Above each one, she added the date of their disappearance. Beginning with the previous March, when Dan King disappeared, there was one missing person reported during the second week of the month for every month except June, November, and February. Everyone looked at the board, stunned.

Gabi sat back down and typed a few keys on her computer. "In February, we had an unexpected winter storm. There was six inches of snow that fell overnight, after four inches of ice. The whole city shut down for days."

She typed a bit more. "In November, we had a late season tornado come through. I remember this because it destroyed so many houses so close to the holidays. The shelters were still overrun when Thanksgiving rolled around. My church did a lot of volunteer work to make sure they had Thanksgiving dinner. In June, we had all the rain and flooding that made it impossible for people to get around anywhere."

Lucy stood up and added the information to the timeline.

"Hmmm," Katie hummed. "How does this fit with a woman/man scorned theory? Surely the timing for someone being turned down doesn't happen on such a precise schedule?"

Again, Gabi spoke up. "I might have an answer for that. Last night, you mentioned several places that some of the men had been to, so I started looking to see if they had any special events going on. The Open Closet is the only one that had anything of significance. The second Tuesday of every month, they used to have drag shows. They advertised them all over the place. When Jimmy disappeared, they changed the schedule to be the second and fourth Thursday of the month. There's one tonight." She shuffled through some of the papers on the table and came up with a flier she had printed from The Open Closet's webpage.

Katie took the flier and looked it over before passing it on to Michael. Sheila was sitting close enough to see the screen where Gabi had pulled up the website again.

Clearing her throat, Sheila said, "That's a great theory. But we've just proven that all the men weren't gay. How would a drag show apply to them?"

Lucy spoke up. "Drag shows bring in a ton of people who aren't gay. It's a popular event with the twenty- and thirty-year-old crowd. They treat it almost like a Broadway play. Singing, dancing, modeling -- what more could you ask for? Add to it a bar with liquor and a dance floor, it's the perfect trifecta."

"That brings up another connection." All eyes shifted to Katie. "Drugs. If Nathan Dixon is dealing drugs, what better place to do so than a crowded bar? He owns the place, so he would know that there's a bigger crowd with more possible customers on these nights. What if these disappearances were over drugs? Either these guys were looking to score something recreationally, or they were witness to a deal and threatened to tell."

Andy turned and wrote the new theory on the board.

"I think there's just one thing left to do." This time, Sheila had center stage. "We go partying." Her statement was met with silence.

"Man, ya'll have all the fun. I have plans I can't cancel tonight," Gabi whined.

"If Gabi can't go, we're short one person. I want us paired up." Michael had taken command.

Feeling the dread build in her stomach, Katie tried not to show her nervousness. She had never been to a club, let alone a gay nightclub. She was raised on a secluded ranch that she'd never stepped foot off of until she left at eighteen. Then she was determined to finish her degrees as soon as possible. She left herself little time for a social life, as she was too busy with volunteer work and holding down a job while going to school full time. She didn't drink and she didn't know how to dance. This plan was sounding more and more like a disaster to her.

"What if we call in Ryan Brewer? Would he come without his partner?" Sheila suggested.

"One way to find out." Michael pulled his phone from his pocket and dialed as Sheila turned to Lucy and Katie.

"Why don't we go shopping and get something to wear? We can get ready at my place, that way you don't have to drive all the way to Nashville."

Katie didn't bother to tell her that she lived just fifteen minutes away in Smyrna. She thought staying occupied in the interim hours would help keep her calm, though. Maybe she could pick up a few tips from the other women. Plan made, they turned to tell Michael where they were going before heading out the door.

Michael ended his call and told them that Ryan would be more than willing to come along -- without Dane. They agreed to pick the ladies up at Sheila's apartment at eight-thirty, as the bar opened at nine and the show started at ten.

Twenty-Two

Michael, Ryan and Andy discussed strategy for the night on their way to pick up the ladies.

"Ryan, you should pair with Sheila and cover the dance floor while Andy and Lucy stay together at the bar. Katie and I will cover the dressing rooms and the stage." Knowing his partner, Michael knew Katie wouldn't be comfortable at either the bar to the dance floor. While she hadn't come right out and said anything, he could sense the tension rolling off her earlier when this plan was hatched.

"Why do you all get to have all the fun?" Andy was trying to rile Michael. Though nothing had ever been said, Andy knew Michael was protective of Katie. He had also guessed at Ryan's attraction to her when the agent inquired about her while the men were making last minute plans for the night. "I think Ryan and Katie should pair up. They look more like a couple. Besides Sheila is more your height, Michael. It would be more plausible for you to partner with her."

Michael's look could have frozen the ocean while Ryan's was puppy-dog grateful. Neither of them responded as they pulled into the driveway of Sheila's home and saw the three women standing on the porch. Andy let out a long, low whistle as Ryan's chin hit the ground. The muscle in Michael's jaw clenched as he tried to control his reaction.

First down the stairs was Lucy who had taken the time to spike her short red hair in every possible direction. She was covered collar-to-toes in black skin-tight leather. Her bad-ass attitude projected into the car.

Second down the stairs was Sheila who had on tight black jeans and a low-cut V-neck t-shirt in a shade of yellow that made her dark skin glow.

But it was the sight of Katie coming down the stairs that stopped all the men in their tracks. Known for her conservative black or gray suits topped with the ever-present bun, her look was now the complete opposite. Her hair hung in waves down to her waist and the teal shirt she wore crossed in the front revealing an astonishing amount of cleavage, while the color made her eyes stand out. It would be interesting to see which caught more attention over the course of the evening. The leather mini-skirt she wore stopped well short of her knees, where long, toned legs ended in heeled sandals that were guaranteed to drop a man at her feet. Top it all off with the inherent sense of shyness that she portrayed with a slight vulnerability and she was a recipe for trouble.

At Ryan's step in her direction, Michael quickly moved in front of him and faced off. Immediately recognizing his protectiveness and not wanting to investigate deeper to see what it meant, Michael said the only thing he could to salvage the situation.

"You better keep her safe tonight. If I see one person pawing at her, you will answer to me." Ryan nodded and Michael turned just in time to see Katie sashay down the sidewalk. She wasn't walking that way on purpose, but the shoes altered her gait to make it the most seductive thing he had ever seen.

Working hard to keep both his tongue and the drool in his mouth, he motioned to the car. "Ladies, you all look beautiful tonight."

Katie and Ryan took the third row seating in the FBI vehicle while Andy and Lucy took the middle row and Sheila climbed into the passenger side. Ryan outlined the plan as they drove toward The Open Closet.

The parking lot of the club was packed by the time they arrived. On the long walk from the back of the lot to the door, Katie found herself being checked out by no fewer than fifteen people -- both men and women. She had to fight the urge to tug at the hemline of her skirt and the top her shirt. Michael received the second most appreciative glances.

As they reached the door, Katie leaned over and whispered

in Michael's ear. "Looks like we're competing for all the attention tonight, handsome. May the best person win." She gave him a saucy wink and hooked her hand in the crook of Ryan's arm as they entered the club. Michael stood dumbstruck for a second and then burst out laughing. It was the first time she had ever teased him and he found he liked it, even if it was her nerves talking.

Katie and Ryan made their way over to the front of the stage and snagged a table on the far right. It was positioned so that they could see the door that led to the dressing rooms and the crowd of people watching the show.

"There's a two drink minimum to occupy the tables --" The words stopped short as the two agents looked up into the face of Sam Blackstone.

Sam gave the same long, low whistle that Andy had when he first saw Katie. "Agent Freeman, I didn't recognize you dressed like that. What brings you here tonight?"

Katie tugged at the hem of her skirt, wishing it were six inches longer -- at a minimum. She would prefer that it reach the floor right about now. "We're conducting surveillance, looking to see if we notice anything suspicious. What are you doing here?"

Julie Mellon

"Jimmy's sister hired me to manage the club. I got the job last week, right before I found out about Franklin. Tonight is my first night and I'm already having a struggle to put things back the way Jimmy ran them. Nathan has no idea how to run a business and he has let so many things go since Jimmy disappeared. Franklin and I used to come here all the time, but back then it was monitored more efficiently and the crowd control was better. Unless the power struggle between Jimmy's sister and Nathan ends soon, my hands are going to be tied. I need permission to spend money on basic safety precautions to reinforce the rules around here but Nathan is tight with the purse strings. That's why I'm out here in person reminding people of the two drink minimum. Since I know it's you, I'll let it slide. Anything in particular I can keep an eye out for?"

Shaking her head, Katie replied, "We're looking at the possibility of drugs being sold here. We're also looking at general behavior, seeing if anyone might display characteristics of a sociopath." Ryan looked at her in astonishment. He didn't understand why she was revealing all this to a potential suspect.

"Well, I don't have the first clue about sociopaths, but I do know we have had an increase in drug sales. It's difficult to control it in an atmosphere like this, but it has been a lot worse the past six months. When I interviewed, that was one of the first things I addressed with Ginger. She was glad to have the perspective of a person who has been a patron since the place opened."

"Thanks, Sam. Let us know if you see any activity. There are a few of us here so we can take care of it."

The minute Sam was out of earshot, Ryan turned to Katie. "Why would you tell him all that? Isn't he a suspect? Have you cleared him from any involvement?"

"Oh, he didn't commit these murders. His behavior and demeanor eliminate him." Katie had learned to observe people from the time she was a small child. The ranch that her mother owned housed various abused women and their children. They were allowed to live on the property provided they met certain conditions. First, they weren't allowed to have sons. No males were allowed on the property at any time. Second, they had to have zero contact with their abusers. Any contact earned them a one-way ticket out the gates. Third, they had to agree to counseling and life skills training. They were to work through the psychological trauma while learning a trade, so that when they did leave they could find employment to provide a better life for themselves and their daughters.

Because of this, Katie had the perfect situation to observe

Julie Mellon

human behavior at its worst and the transition people went through when their lives change. She learned to recognize courage, pain, fear, deceit, and many more emotions and how they played out in human expressions and behavior. It was a skill that gave her an advantage in reading potential suspects. It was also something that Michael had picked up on early in their partnership without even needing to ask her about.

Katie felt a twinge of sadness not to have Michael by her side. She had grown accustomed to their dynamic and missed the familiarity of his easy banter. The thoughts of her time on the ranch and the secret she was keeping from him chased away the sadness and replaced it with guilt.

Before she could explain all this to Ryan, Sam reappeared and set two drinks in front of them. "Non-alcoholic and on the house. I instructed the bartender to keep them coming your way when he sees they're almost empty. No one will know the difference." Shooting Katie a wink, he turned and continued walking through the tables checking on the other patrons.

Katie had never seen a drag show before and when it started, she was so caught up in the performances that the third performer was on stage before she remembered to look around. The show started with all the evening's performers onstage in a

Rockettes/Vegas lounge-type number. The second was a solo performance of one of Whitney Houston's most famous songs. The singer's ability to hit the high notes was quite impressive.

Finally dragging her eyes away from a mediocre rendition of a Katy Perry song, Katie realized that the bar had doubled in occupancy. The beat of the dance floor on the upper level was barely discernible, but she did see Michael leaning on the railing looking in her direction. She ran her hand over her hair in their predetermined signal that all was fine and he turned his back, grabbed Sheila's hand and dragged her onto the dance floor. Her momentary pang of jealousy was squashed by the thrill of feeling Ryan take her hand under the table. She was confused by her reaction to two different men, but pushed both aside in order to concentrate on her assignment.

Catching Lucy's eye from where she was perched on a barstool, Katie saw her put her hand to her chest and tilt her head to the left. Realizing she was using the hand-to-the-chest signal to let Katie and Ryan know something was up, Katie moved her eyes to the left in the direction Lucy indicated with her head. About halfway between the sets of agents, at the edge of the seating area for the show and the standing-room-only bar, was a cluster of three men. Katie watched as a white envelope was passed from one hand, while a second envelope was returned.

The third man stood surveying the crowd, watching to see if anyone was observing them. Unfortunately for him, his eyes didn't roam out far enough to see Katie watching.

As the three began to disband, Lucy moved to intercept the lookout, Andy moved to stop the buyer, and Katie and Ryan moved into the path of the seller. It all happened quietly and in less than twenty seconds. The four agents ushered the men toward the door that led backstage. Sam saw them coming and opened the door, leading them into his new office.

Of the three, the seller was the easiest to crack. He was just a college kid looking to make a little money to help pay his tuition. It didn't take much pressure to get him to spill his guts and learn that Nathan was the mastermind behind the operation. In exchange for the agents agreeing not to prosecute, they agreed to give testimony against Nathan. The two were banned from the club until they could show Sam proof of having attended three meetings with a drug counselor. The buyer was simply trying to score a fix and a squad car was called to take him downtown.

Similar scenarios played out three more times before midnight. Between the six agents and the narcotics detectives that had been called in, they had the names of ten people who indicated Nathan as the leader of the drug ring. Following the last set of people they rounded up, Michael stepped out of Sam's office and caught sight of Nathan stepping through a door further down the hall. He ducked back inside the office and signaled to Katie, Sheila and Ryan to follow him.

Leading the way down the hall, Michael rapped sharply on the door.

"Enter," came the command from inside.

"I thought you didn't come to the club while it was open," Michael greeted Nathan as he walked into the office.

"Oh, you know, I'm just checking on our new manager. Making sure things are running smoothly. What brings you down here?" Nobody missed the appreciative look he cast over Katie -- of course the second scan up and down her body was difficult to overlook.

"Allow me to introduce my partner. This is Special Agent Freeman. Also working with us this evening is Detective Reynolds from the MPD and Special Agent Brewer." Michael indicated each person in turn and smirked at the sour twist of Nathan's mouth when he learned that all of them were law enforcement.

"If you're here investigating, you're in the wrong place. There's nothing illegal going on in my bar." He was defensive and his denial was just icing on the cake of his guilt. His immediate assumption that they were there investigating something illegal and the beads of sweat on his brow gave him away.

"Funny that you should mention that," Katie said. "I have a list of ten people here who have given sworn testimony that you're the one in charge of the sale of pharmaceuticals happening in this place."

There were so many ticks that appeared in his body language that Katie's innate ability to ready people wasn't needed. Nathan began tapping his fingers on the desk and judging from the trembles in his body, he was bouncing his leg underneath. He began to look around the office, anywhere but where the law enforcement officers were standing. Finally there was his unconvincing denial. "Um…well, ah…I don't know what they told you, but I have nothing to do with drugs."

Michael nudged Sheila forward, indicating for her to make the arrest. "Mr. Dixon, we have enough evidence against you to place you under arrest. Please stand and put your hands behind your back."

Nathan slumped in his chair before doing as instructed. Sheila read him his rights and they led him out of the office, through the back door and into the hands of the narcotics officers.

It was just after one a.m. and the six decided to call it a

night. They agreed to meet at nine in the conference room to discuss what they'd learned. Katie extended an invitation to Ryan to join them, which earned her a scowl from Michael.

Twenty-Three

It was a very quiet and sleepy crew that filtered into the conference room on Friday morning. Katie entered carrying coffee for everyone and a massive sweet tea from her new favorite drive thru. She ignored the smirk Michael directed her way as she handed out the specialized drink orders, noting that someone else had already had the thought. There were cups in everyone's hands and a large sweet tea sitting on the table.

Andy gratefully reached up and took the coffee from Katie. "Thanks. I need to double up on caffeine today. I'm getting too old to stay out so late." There were murmured agreements around the table.

They all sat in silence for a few long minutes; the only sound was the sighing of deep yawns. Gabi had turned on the coffee pot before anyone arrived and the smell of brewing coffee seeped into their senses as they indulged in the calorie and sugar-ladened drinks Katie and Michael had provided. Ryan was the last person to arrive and he came bearing three dozen donuts fresh from the bakery down the street.

"Oh god, I knew I loved you," Lucy nearly swooned at Ryan's feet as he sat a box right in front of her. She slapped several hands that tried to invade the box and only surrendered them when she had grabbed the three she wanted. Then she saw Andy

Free to Deceive

looking at her.

"Don't look at me that way. I'm a big girl, I need a lot to get me going." Still looking at him, Lucy defiantly shoved half the donut in her mouth. The others laughed at her antics and as the sugar began flowing in their bloodstream, they began planning for the next steps.

Being the only one who had gotten a full night's sleep, Gabi started the meeting. "I ran background checks on the men and women y'all arrested last night. Most of them were clean. Two of the dealers had prior charges for drug possession, but nothing big enough to warrant distribution charges. I was really shocked by that because the narcotics guys were adamant that Nathan was a big-time dealer. All we got last night were small-time charges. In fact the ones you cut deals with were so small-time that they didn't even know you didn't have enough to really do any harm to them."

"What time did you get in this morning?" Katie asked Gabi.

"I've been here since about seven, maybe a little before. But I did get home and in bed by ten last night. If I had known ya'll were still at the club, I might've come and joined you.

"Oh, and I cross-referenced the people from last night with our victims -- nada. I'm still in the middle of compiling all the credit card records for all the victims now that I've completed the background checks on all the suspects."

"Did you find anything interesting on Jack Patterson?" Katie was interested to see if he was as sleazy as he seemed.

"Not really. His driving record is clean, which isn't surprising considering his job requires that. He uses his credit cards liberally and is definitely living beyond his means. Of course, that could be because car sales have been down for the past few years. He's spent money in nearly every store in The Avenue. The one interesting thing I did find is that he frequently travels to Knoxville."

Michael was the first to break the resulting silence. "Was he there near the time of Kelly and Chad's disappearances? I've been thinking it was time for us to go to Knoxville and look for a connection. Maybe this is it."

Gabi turned back to her spreadsheet and looked at the information she had pulled from Jack's credit card statements. "Hmm, he was there the first week of July and it looks like he rented a cabin in Gatlinburg the last week of November that I can track. There's a receipt from a gas station halfway between Knoxville and here on the second Monday of November, so it looks like he came back from vacation that week. Do we know the exact date Kelly or Chad disappeared?"

Sheila flipped through the file they had received from the

Free to Deceive

Knox County sheriff's department on Kelly Porter. "It looks like he made it through the Fourth of July holiday but didn't report to work on the seventh. He was off the day before, so there isn't a definite timeframe for his disappearance. Could have been Monday night after he got off work, any time during the day on Tuesday, or early Wednesday morning before he didn't show up for work."

"What about his vehicle? Was it ever found?" Katie asked. "It might give us a clue to his activities on the days prior."

Sheila dug back into the folder while Michael grabbed the file for Chad Montgomery's disappearance and began looking for the same information.

"There is no mention of the vehicle at all," she said.

"No mention in Chad's case either," Michael added.

"Looks like you need someone to go to Knoxville." Ryan spoke for the first time since the meeting began. "I'm available if you need me to go."

Katie and Michael exchanged a look across the table that no one missed.

"Look, I know what you think of my partner. Quite frankly, I agree. But, I'm the junior man on the totem pole. Eventually one of us will be reassigned, hopefully before I kill him. Please don't lump me in with him. Besides, he took a few days off rather than be grounded for his behavior the other day. I'd really like to help out." Ryan looked sincere as he said this, trying to get everyone there to stop associating him with his partner's attitude. He didn't hold the same views and he took all his cases seriously. He knew that their closure rate wouldn't be what it was without his own investigative skills. He also knew it could be higher if Dane would stop acting like an ass.

Knowing what it's like to be saddled with a bad partner simply for being new, Katie felt bad for Ryan. "I'll go with you. Michael can stay here and finish the interviews with Sheila."

Michael started to protest, but the look Katie directed him stopped the words from leaving his mouth. They stared each other down before Michael finally blinked. "Okay, but drive safely and call me when you head back." He nodded at Ryan as the two left the room. When he refocused on the others around the table, they were all staring at him -- Andy had his eyebrows raised.

"What?" Michael knew he sounded defensive, but he didn't like his partner working with anyone else, especially when it involved traveling to a different city. He liked knowing she was safe and he really hoped that Ryan didn't try to pull any moves he might have learned from Dane.

Free to Deceive

The others quickly looked away and Sheila picked up the stack of folders that represented the interviews they had yet to complete.

Twenty-Four

The drive to Knoxville started out slightly awkward. Katie wasn't good with casual conversation and Ryan was naturally quiet. When he started the car, country music blared out of the speakers. *That's different. I guess I've gotten used to Michael's classic rock.* Immediately pushing thoughts of Michael out of her head, she turned her attention to Ryan.

"So you like country music?" she asked.

"Oh, yeah. I was born and raised in these parts. You can't be from Music City and not like country. What do you listen to? I can change it if it bothers you."

Katie shook her head. "I was raised on oldies, you know, classic '60s and '70s stuff. I don't listen to music now, just what's on the radio in Michael's car. When I'm in mine, I have on talk radio. I'm fine with whatever."

Ryan lowered the volume a little and they lapsed into silence again.

They were twenty miles down the highway before Ryan spoke again. "Why did you come with me? Better yet, why did you allow me to go?"

"I know what it's like to get stuck with a bad partner."

"That's it? That's all you're going to say? I thought Michael was a good guy. He has a good reputation." Ryan quickly

Free to Deceive

glanced over as he asked.

"Oh, Michael's fantastic -- well, other than teasing me and getting me hooked on food I shouldn't be eating." Katie laughed, thinking of her partner.

Realizing that Ryan was frowning, it dawned on her that she didn't answer his question about a bad partner. "My partner in Louisiana was a nightmare. In fact, the first time I met Dane, he made me think of Grady. He had the ability to be a good investigator, but he didn't care to put in the effort. He was quick to take the credit for my work. He loved media interviews, which made it difficult to keep aspects of the case quiet. I used to think he had a way of notifying the press so that they arrived at crime scenes before we did. He had this little flourish he would do as he stepped under crime scene tape. It reminded me of a bad cop drama on TV."

"You watch TV, but don't listen to music?" Ryan was amused by this piece of information.

Katie turned red. "I was addicted during college. I don't go out much, so when I have down time, I like to binge watch any show dealing with crime. I really like the ones that recount true crime."

He laughed at her embarrassment, but the more she opened up, the more he liked her. He wanted to keep her talking just to hear her, so he started asking her questions. "Is your former partner the reason you came to Tennessee?"

As Katie answered the questions, Ryan slowly learned which topics were sensitive and which ones made her laugh. Her family was off limits. Other than saying she was raised in Arizona, she gave no indication of any other details. Wanting to make her comfortable, he avoided topics that put her on guard and worked to keep her talking. Before they knew it, they were pulling up to the Knox County Sheriff's Office.

Deputy Gillard came out to greet them once they introduced themselves to the officer manning the front desk. She was a tall woman with red hair that was pulled back into a bun that matched the one Katie wore. Directing them back to her desk, she produced the files for both Chad Montgomery and Kelly Porter.

"I investigated both of these disappearances. I didn't see anything that would connect them at the time. I still don't see anything after reviewing the files. The guys were just there one day and gone the next." The confused look on her face was mixed with frustration at having missed something and still not being able to find the missing link.

"Do you have any information on their vehicles?" Katie asked. Ryan was content to sit back and let Katie ask all the questions. He was thankful for the opportunity to work with someone besides Dane and was taking the approach of easing into the situation.

"Hmmm," Gillard said, flipping through the file, "there isn't anything noted in the file regarding vehicles. Let me pull up DMV files." Turning to her computer, she pulled up the registration for the vehicles in the two men's names.

"Looks like Montgomery drove a red Jeep Grand Cherokee, three years old. It was sitting in the parking lot where he parked for work." A few clicks later, she found the information for Porter. "Looks like he drove a Ford pick-up. It was found at the base of the zip line tower he was supposed to operate that morning. His keys and cell phone were inside, but that wasn't unusual. They used walkie-talkies when on the zip line, it was more reliable."

Katie sat in thought for a few seconds, tapping her fingers against her bottom lip.

Finally, Ryan asked, "Is there any connection between either of them and the Nashville or Murfreesboro area?"

"Kelly Porter dated a woman named Keri Eldridge throughout college -- they both went to MTSU. He moved back to Knoxville after graduation, but she stayed here. He was known to go visit her occasionally even though they broke up several years ago.

They remained friends. We called her when he disappeared to see if she had heard from him, but she said it had been a few weeks since he called."

The minute Keri's name was mentioned, both Katie and Ryan sat straight up and looked at each other in astonishment.

"What? What did I say?" Gillard had no idea which part of her statement had inspired such a reaction.

"Keri Eldridge was dating one of our other victims," Katie finally explained. She pulled out her cell phone and called Michael to give him an update.

"Michael and Sheila are going to go back and talk to Keri again. Let's see if there is anyone else here we can talk to." Turning back to Deputy Gillard, Katie thanked her for her time. They shook hands and the agents turned to leave.

From the station, they grabbed a quick lunch and went to the admissions office at the university and talked to Chad Montgomery's coworkers and boss. None of them added anything more to what they knew. Deciding to switch gears and interview Kelly's twin, they headed toward the mountains and the zip line company in search of Kyle Porter.

When they arrived at the office, the only person present was a wilderness guide who had just returned from a week-long trip through the mountainside. "Can I help you?" she greeted them.

"We're looking for Kyle Porter." Ryan stepped forward and presented his ID.

"Oh, this must be about Kelly. Kyle is on an overnight trip with a group of tourists. He won't be reachable until morning. They're due to return around ten. Is there anything I can answer for you?"

They stayed and talked to the guide for a while, learning more about Kelly's habits and the business. Unfortunately, she wasn't able to shed any light about who might have murdered him. Thanking her for her time, they drove the hour back to Knoxville and checked into a hotel before heading out to dinner.

Katie pulled out her phone to call Michael and let him know that she was delayed in returning, but would be back the next afternoon.

Twenty-Five

Once Katie and Ryan left for Knoxville, Michael and Sheila went through the files to make a list of people they should talk to. List in hand, they headed out to The Avenue. They spent all afternoon talking to the employees and managers of the various shops where the victims worked, ending at the steakhouse.

The manager on duty was the one working the night Franklin failed to show up for his shift. "He was always reliable. I hired him when he was sixteen. His official title was host, but he never failed to pitch in where needed. He would bus the tables, wash the dishes, make the food -- at least the food that didn't require operating machinery. He was underage and not legally able to touch any of it. He was a great kid."

"Mr. Simms, can you tell us if there were any other employees that were close to Franklin?" Sheila was asking the questions so far. A part of her was proud that Michael showed enough faith in her skills to allow her to take the lead. The other part of her was worried that he was just standing back and evaluating her performance.

"I don't think there was an employee here that didn't like Franklin. Even as he was entrusted with more responsibility, he still assisted where he could. He was known for carrying heavy trays for some of the other servers. Take Kristen, for example.

Free to Deceive

She's seven months pregnant and being on her feet for a whole shift is difficult. He made sure to carry most of her trays out, while still maintaining his own section. It was to the point that when we made up the schedules, we would make sure he was assigned a section closest to the person who needed the most assistance. Otherwise, Franklin would run himself ragged trying to be everywhere at once. But he never lost his smile."

"Is it possible to talk to the servers who were scheduled for the same shift that day?"

"Well, let's see…" Mr. Simms checked the schedule hanging on the wall of his office. "Abbie Griffin is here today. I can see if she has a few minutes. Susanne Hodgins took the weekend off. She went to Knoxville to visit her family. Her next shift is Monday, but I can give you her cell phone number if you want to call her."

Michael thanked him as Mr. Simms went out to see if Abbie could come in for a minute.

"Too bad we didn't think of interviewing the servers the other day. Susanne was the woman who hit on you the entire time we ate lunch. You could have played that up to get some information out of her," Sheila teased Michael.

He rolled his eyes just as the office door opened and Abbie walked in. She was a short, slender woman whose personality

166

seemed to bubble out of her. When she spoke, it sounded like she had just inhaled a tank of helium.

"Mr. Simms said you wanted to see me?" Her wide hazel eyes looked back and forth between the two agents.

Sheila resumed her role as the lead investigator. "We were wondering if you could walk us through the day of Franklin's disappearance. Just tell us what you remember."

"Of course. Well, I was supposed to be at work at four. I'm chronically late, so my boyfriend has taken to setting my alarm thirty minutes early. That was the first day of the experiment, so I was actually about ten minutes early for my shift. Talk about a first! When I got here, there were only about four empty spots in the lot. I parked near the back, in the closest of the vacant spots. I had to walk past Franklin's Mazda. We all make fun of it because it needs a paint job. The front passenger quarter panel is primer, the back bumper is red. We think the original color of the car was either blue or silver, but it's so faded you couldn't really tell. Franklin had it so long he didn't really remember the original color either. But he loved that car -- said as long as it ran, he was going to drive it. Anyway, it was parked about three spots up from mine."

"Do you remember anyone else in the lot, or any other cars pulling in?"

Free to Deceive

"I don't think so. But I was so happy to be early and have a chance to get my section together that I didn't really pay much attention. I just knew that I was going to surprise everyone. I came in and started wrapping silverware in napkins. When I headed out to start the transfer of services from the lunch server, I noticed that Franklin was nowhere to be found. I mentioned it to Mr. Simms and he went to check the bathroom and kitchens. I took over my section and it was about thirty minutes before I found out Franklin really wasn't here."

"So you didn't see Susanne clock in?"

Abbie laughed. "No, but then again, we aren't exactly best friends."

Exchanging looks with Sheila, Michael asked the next question. "What do you mean?"

"Oh, I probably shouldn't have said anything, but she's a bit strange. She's extremely shy when it comes to conversation, but you put her out on the floor and she puts on this personality that's a little embarrassing. She goes over the top by flirting with the customers, often inappropriately. There have been several complaints about her. We even have repeat customers who request any section but hers. It's hard to explain, but it's like she doesn't get social etiquette."

"She was our server the other day, so I understand what you

mean," Michael commiserated with Abbie. He was trying to make her comfortable enough to say more.

"So you really do get it. Mr. Simms asked me to try to mentor her. I tried, really I did. But she wasn't willing to listen or to learn. She got hostile about it, and in case you didn't notice, she's a bit bigger than me. I finally had to tell Mr. Simms that it was a lost cause." Abbie shook her head with regret. "Anyway, I really need to get back to my customers, is there anything else I can answer for you?"

Not having any more questions, they let her go back to work. Michael then grabbed his phone and called Susanne. He arranged to meet with her for an interview at nine on Monday morning. She was due for the lunch shift at eleven.

Michael and Sheila called it a day around five. As he was driving back to his house in Smyrna, Michael thought over the day. He still didn't like that Katie was in Knoxville with a practical stranger. It took all his strength to stop himself from calling to check in on her. Now that he was alone, he examined how he reacted to her. He couldn't deny that how he felt toward her was different than the sisterly feelings he tried to make them out to be. Maybe he should encourage her to date Ryan, at least then there would be a reason to squash his

Free to Deceive

attraction, besides that she was his partner.

When she first transferred to Tennessee, their boss was suspicious that her reassignment was due to an inappropriate relationship with her former partner. Michael had asked her about it, point blank. She denied it and said she had a rule about dating or sleeping with colleagues. He believed her when she said it.

As he was pulling into his driveway, his phone rang. Looking at the display, he saw Candice's name come up on the screen. Staying with Candice was about more than just sparing her feelings; it was also a way to keep him from acknowledging his feelings for Katie. He took a deep breath and answered, though he really wanted to decline the call.

Silently cursing himself for being a nice guy, he greeted his soon-to-be-ex-girlfriend -- if he could just work up the nerve to break her heart. "Hey, Candice. What's up?"

"I'm off work early. You want to take me to dinner?" He used to like how her voice turned sultry over the phone when she was trying to spend time with him. Now the sound of her cooing made him want to hang up.

Taking mental inventory of what was in his refrigerator at home and realizing it was sadly deficient in anything truly edible, he agreed to pick her up at six-thirty.

Julie Mellon

Michael knew the night was off to a bad start when he reacted to Candice's appearance with annoyance instead of appreciation. She hadn't changed over the course of their relationship - he had. Coming down the stairs from her second floor apartment, the first thing Michael saw were the stiletto heels on her perfectly pedicured feet. Her bare legs extended for miles up to the tube dress that stopped mid-thigh and clung to every curve. The dress was strapless and Candice's blonde hair hung in waves down to her shoulders. She kept herself in great physical condition and she looked fabulous in what she was wearing.

All Michael saw was a triplet to Keri and Missy and it made him wonder how superficial his life was. Thinking back over the past year of their relationship, he realized they had never had a serious conversation -- he didn't know her political beliefs, or what she wanted to do with her life, or if she wanted marriage and children. In fact, he couldn't really even recall what they did talk about when they were out.

Walking around to the passenger side of the car, Michael opened the door for her and told her she looked beautiful before helping her in and closing the door behind her. The beaming smile she directed at him made his heart sink.

Free to Deceive

"Where would you like to go?" Michael normally put thought into dates that he planned, but since this was a last minute outing, he deferred to Candice.

Pursing her lips, she gave the idea some thought and then named off one of the more popular restaurants in Nashville that played country music and also had a dance floor in the center. He wasn't really in the mood to be around a lot of people and he especially didn't relish the idea of spending time in a loud, overcrowded pseudo- dance club, but since he had asked her opinion, he gave her a tight smile and pulled out of the lot. Candice didn't notice, she was too busy checking her reflection in the mirror over the visor.

"Candy, you made it!" The squeal came from a shorter version of Candice as they entered the restaurant. "The rest of the gang is all here. Our table is to the left, about mid-way down the dance floor."

Seeing the surprise on Michael's face, Candice hurriedly explained. "My friends wanted to have a get-together tonight. You never come when we hang out, you're always too busy. You need to get out and have some fun once in a while." She pouted and rubbed her breasts against his arm as she talked.

An hour later, Michael was fighting a headache of epic proportions. Two nights in a row in a club was more than he was used to. And he had to admit to himself that he had enjoyed dancing with Sheila more than he had with Candice or her friends. What made it worse was that each of her girlfriends that he danced with made obvious remarks about him proposing to Candice soon. He knew he was going to have to do something about the break-up sooner rather than later.

He had just sat down at the table from his recent trip around the dance floor with one of her friends that he thought was named Sandy when he felt his phone vibrate. As he pulled it from his pocket, Candice snatched it from his hand.

"We're having fun tonight. No phones allowed." She tried to tuck it into the top of her dress, but Michael grabbed it back before it made it that far.

"I'm a law enforcement officer. I investigate crimes, including murder. They don't stop simply because I'm out to dinner. You've known for a year that my job doesn't come with nine to five hours."

The others around the table stopped to stare. One of the other men looked at him with relief. Michael and he had shared a few common looks and he knew he wasn't the only one trying to end a fiasco of a relationship.

Looking at his phone, he saw a text from Katie.

Free to Deceive

Kyle is unavailable for an interview until morning. We are grabbing a hotel room for the night. We should be back no later than three tomorrow afternoon. - Katie

Why so late? -MP

He is on an overnight expedition with a few tourists. Won't be back until 10. -KF

Good luck and drive safe. - MP

Michael tucked the phone back in his pocket, any semblance of a good mood evaporating on the spot. One glance at Candice's face was enough to let him know that things were about to get worse.

Candice had never met Katie, but she saw her once from the window of the bed and breakfast that Michael's sister owned. They were complete opposites and Candice had no reason to be jealous, as Katie had only been his partner for a week at that point. But she took one look at Katie and hated her on sight. Candice had harped on his partnership with her ever since, even going so far as to demand he get a new partner.

"You like her better than me. Are you sleeping with her?

She wears a bun, for heaven's sake." Candice's claws were coming out. Michael hated drama and he hated a public scene even more. Candice was winding up for a massive public tantrum. Even worse, he could sense her friends closing rank.

"Look, Katie is my partner. She's in Knoxville interviewing people for our investigation. She was just texting me to let me know that she needed to stay overnight. It's standard protocol. And I don't date or sleep with my colleagues. She's my partner and she is a brilliant investigator. I'm not requesting to work with anyone else, so you need to get over this jealousy." Michael kept his voice quiet, but by the time he finished his speech, Candice nearly had smoke coming out her ears.

"I'm done being the nice, patient girlfriend. Either you propose to me now and give up this crazy job, or we're through. You could join your family's business. I know you could take control of it in no time."

Michael sat in stunned silence for a few minutes. She had made a few remarks over the past few months about him working for the family business, but he hadn't realized that she was fantasizing and recreating his entire life. And he was even more surprised that she considered herself a patient girlfriend.

"I love my job. I plan to do it for the rest of my life, as long as I am able. I have no interest in working for the

Free to Deceive

family business -- especially as the head of it. My cousin Joey does a fantastic job of making it a success. And I have no intention of proposing to you, tonight or ever. I don't intend for that to sound mean, but you know we've been having problems for months. I even broke things off a few months ago. I'm not quite sure how we ended up back together, but this isn't working for me. This is a conversation I've wanted to have with you in private for some time, but you always manage to keep us from ever being alone. Well, you started it here, so I'm finishing it here. Do you want me to take you home, or can you find your own ride?"

He knew he sounded childish with the 'you started it' line, but he just couldn't stop the words while he was on a roll. She didn't seem to get the message when he said it a few months ago one-on-one; perhaps she would now that he said it in front of her friends.

"You can't do this to me. We're getting married. I already have my dress picked out and my bridesmaids lined up." Her eyes filled with tears and Michael had a difficult time not letting his 'nice guy' come to the rescue.

"I'm sorry, Candice. We are *not* getting married. I'm not in love with you and you have some maturing to do before you're ready to head down the aisle. You are a thirty-year-old woman who wants to do nothing more than go out and party. That isn't me. It's why I don't hang out with your friends. My idea of a good night is staying home watching a movie, or having the guys over for a poker night occasionally. We just aren't meant to be. I wish you luck finding what you need."

Michael looked over at the guy he had connected with and tilted his head toward Candice, silently asking if he could see her home. At his returned nod, Michael put a couple twenties on the table to cover their drinks and dinner and then left the restaurant, leaving a sobbing Candice in the arms of her girlfriends. He felt like an ass for leaving the way he had, but she had pushed the issue and he had taken the opportunity to finally break free of the relationship.

Twenty-Six

After checking in to a hotel on the outskirts of Knoxville and texting with Michael, Katie went down to the lobby to meet Ryan. They planned to walk next door and have dinner at the Mexican restaurant that adjoined the hotel parking lot. The more they were together the more she liked him. He was a nice guy who had goals in life. He loved working missing persons cases, but wished that he didn't have the partner that he did. He was serious and loved to read -- almost as much as she did. Dinner passed with them debating the merits of the classics and which was better, science fiction or romance. She was surprised to find that he had read a fair share of romance novels -- and even more surprised that he would admit it. They both shared a love of the mystery/suspense genre and read several of the same authors. Katie couldn't remember the last time she had such a great evening and had to keep telling herself that it wasn't a date. For once, the entire evening passed without her comparing Ryan to Michael.

When he walked her back to her hotel room, he slowly leaned down and brushed a kiss across her cheek. She smiled shyly and lowered her gaze to the floor.

"Good night. I enjoyed our dinner," Ryan said quietly. Then he turned and went to the next door in the hall.

Julie Mellon

Katie finally looked over and replied, "Good night. I did too." She slowly closed the door behind her and put the safety chain in place.

They met in the lobby Saturday morning and grabbed a bagel and muffin from the continental breakfast bar that was set up for guests. Heading over to the zip line office one more time, they arrived just as Kyle was unlocking the door with a group of very dirty and tired-looking campers behind him.

"Can I help you folks?" he asked as they walked up to the trailer that served as the office.

"I'm Special Agent Katie Freeman and this is my partner Special Agent Ryan Brewer. We'd like a few minutes to talk to you about your brother."

The affable smile drained from his face and he nodded. "Give me a few minutes to process the guests and get the gear sorted. Shouldn't take more than twenty minutes." The campers looked at the agents curiously as they filed in behind Kyle.

The woman they talked to the previous day showed up shortly after that and took over processing the gear. Kyle came over to them ten minutes later and they sat at a picnic table in front of the office.

Free to Deceive

"My parents and I are trying to plan a funeral for Kelly. Any idea when we'll be able to have his remains?" Kyle was holding his emotions at bay, but exhaustion clung to him and seemed to run deeper than just that caused by an overnight camping trip.

"I can check with Dr. Bennett and see if she has an idea of when that might be," Katie started gently. "Can you tell us about Kelly? Did he often go to Murfreesboro? Do you know if he had plans to go there the few days he was off?"

"Kelly was still madly in love with Keri. She was his girlfriend through college." Seeing that they knew whom he was talking about, he continued. "She had moved on, but he never gave up hope. He kept trying to win her back. I don't know if he planned to go those few days, but that isn't unusual. He didn't clear his schedule with me. But since his car was here that morning, doesn't that mean that if he did go he returned from there?"

Ryan answered, "Not necessarily. The person who killed him could have returned his vehicle."

He exchanged a look with Katie as he said this. How had his vehicle appeared at work? If his killer drove it all the way from Murfreesboro, how did they get back? And if the killer did drive it, was it processed for prints?

"Where is his vehicle now?" Katie was ready to have words with the local authorities if no one had processed the vehicle.

Kyle waved to the parking lot. There was a company logo on the side of the truck that was in the lot. "It's a company truck, so several of us drive it. The sheriff's department took prints from inside, but said they were of no help."

Relieved that an attempt had been made to collect evidence, Katie made note of it in the file. She briefly wondered why the information wasn't in the file that Deputy Gillard had turned over yesterday.

"Did you or your brother know a Chad Montgomery?"

Kyle thought for a second. "I don't think so. He might have been a customer, though. I can check our insurance waivers and see if he ever signed one."

Katie nodded and they waited while Kyle went into the office and pulled up the records. He returned several minutes later and shook his head. "We have no record of a Chad Montgomery coming here in the past three years."

Thanking him for his time, they promised to get back to him regarding his brother's remains and began the drive back to Murfreesboro.

Calling ahead to let Michael know their expected time of

Free to Deceive

arrival, they scheduled a meeting for three o'clock. Everyone was in the conference room when Katie and Ryan arrived and they got straight to the point of recounting what they had learned.

Michael and Sheila reviewed their interviews with the employees. Gabi recapped the security footage she was reviewing from the stores, and Ryan went over the interviews from Knoxville.

They tossed around the idea of how Kelly's car could have been in the lot in Knoxville if he had been kidnapped and murdered in Murfreesboro. Adding in the fact that Chad Montgomery's car was also found at his place of business in Knoxville, the scenario was even stranger.

"It lends credibility to the idea of two people working together," Michael said.

Nodding, Katie agreed. "Yes, but the fact that the vehicles of all thirteen were found at or near their places of employment leads me to assume that the killer didn't know all of them that well. It also makes me think, discounting the two in Knoxville, that the killer is very familiar with a *place* that they all frequented, not necessarily them as a person.

They were quiet for a few minutes, Katie doodling on the paper in front of her as her mind spun through what they knew of the various activities. Sheila was flipping her pen up in the air, while Michael was pacing in front of the dry erase boards.

Finally turning to face everyone, Michael decided to call it a day. "Let's head home. Why don't we all take a share of the security footage and look it over on our own computers tomorrow. We can start fresh Monday morning." He figured they had been running at full-speed all week and one day of rest would help them recharge.

Twenty-Seven

Katie went to church with the Shoulders family, owners the bed and breakfast that she called home. It was rare that she had a Sunday morning free to spend with the three children, even though she really enjoyed having them around. Little Carrie had turned four the previous week and was excited about being a big girl. The family had made a big deal out of removing the side railing on her twin bed that protected her from falling out in the middle of the night. In truth, it could have been removed a lot sooner, but it was a tradition they had started with their oldest, Ian. After church, they returned to the house and Katie made several batches of her mother's chocolate chip cookies.

In all the years since she left the ranch, Katie always found solace in making the cookies. She could feel her mother's presence as she mixed the dough and pulled the finished product out of the oven. Reliving those memories today made her mad. She didn't like thinking of how her mother had deceived her all these years.

Grabbing a plate and loading it down with cookies, Katie left to go visit her mother's cousin, Billy Sheppard. Billy was the reason Katie was forced to keep secrets from her partner.

When she was first partnered with Michael, he had handed her three cold case files, one of which was the murder of Hank

Stephens. He had been found shot to death in his home with excess levels of alcohol and OxyContin in his system. His wife, Charlene, was nowhere to be found. On the same night Hank had been killed, Billy Sheppard was arrested for attempting to sell a large quantity of OxyContin to an undercover officer. With Billy locked up, he was never a suspect in the murder, but there was suspicion that he had sold the drugs to Hank's wife, allowing her to drug him, shoot him and disappear. Katie had thought the case strange from the beginning. Why would she drug and then shoot him? Why not wait until he fell asleep to shoot him? It was even stranger once she met Billy.

The first time she walked up on his porch with Michael, he nearly fell out of his rickety chair. He had been stringing beans and his hand shook so badly she wanted to reach over and take the knife from his hand. He denied his reaction, which only made Katie more suspicious. She waited until the case she was working on wrapped up, then she made a batch of her cookies and then went to talk to him.

Katie didn't know anything about her history. She and her mother had lived on the ranch since before Katie was born. Given her mother's tendency to help abused women, Katie suspected that her mother had been abused herself and hidden from the world. She figured if her father were that bad of a man, she didn't

Free to Deceive

want to know him and she had never bothered to try to locate him. But she knew her mother had a southern accent that hadn't faded with time, probably due to her lack of interaction with other people in Arizona.

When she had shown up on Billy's porch, he again tried to deny his initial reaction to Katie. But one bite of the cookies and he caved. Charlene had always made the cookies for him -- she added a secret ingredient to them that altered the flavor and made them the best chocolate chip cookies in the world. Once he admitted that he recognized the cookies, he told Katie that she looked exactly like Charlene Stephens. Katie had put two and two together and deduced that her mother, Sarah Freeman, was Charlene Stephens.

Billy talked all that afternoon about Charlene's upbringing and how close they were. He was glad to know that she was all right. She had promised to let him know she made it safely to her destination, but he had spent two years in prison on the drug charges and had missed any communication she might have tried to send him. He never talked to Katie about the murder of Hank.

Today, she was determined to get him to talk about it.

As usual, Billy was sitting on his front porch; this time he was peeling potatoes. In the few weeks since she had been there, he had propped up the sagging right side of the porch and looked to be making renovations to the rest of the run down house.

"Good afternoon," she greeted him, placing the plate of cookies beside him.

He finished peeling the potato he was working on and dropped it in the bucket of water next to his chair. He told her the water kept the potatoes from turning brown in the air once they were peeled.

Taking the first bite of a cookie, he let out a sigh. "Mmmm, these are still the best damn cookies in the world. And you're as good at making them as your mother was."

Katie's emotions warred with each other. She was eager to know more about her mother's past, but she was desperate to know about her father's murder. She couldn't keep living with the secret without knowing if it was possible that her mother was a murderer. Katie was still careful not to mention her mother's new name or where she was living. She didn't feel like it was her responsibility to reveal her secrets. Also, if anyone ever found out that her mother was Charlene Stephens, she didn't want to put Billy in the position of having to lie.

"How did my mother meet my father?"

Billy's face scrunched up in distaste. "That old bastard

went to school with your mother. She was as beautiful as you are and he wanted her for himself. He was a football player and really popular. Your mom was shy and bookish, but she was a looker. He decided that she would be his. Well, your momma's dad was a mean drunk and he took his anger out on her and her mom. Charlene wanted a way out. When Hank came asking to marry her right after graduation, she took the chance. I always thought she would go to college and get out of this place. Hank put a stop to all that."

Figuring that he would never approach the subject, she decided to be blunt. "Do you think she killed him?"

"Do *you* think she did?" Billy looked right at her as he threw the question back.

"I have never witnessed a mean action from her. She was always gentle, but desperate women can do some unexpected things."

Billy looked at her intently for a few seconds. "She was desperate. But there's no way she hurt him. She came to me a few days before she left asking for help to get out of here. She had prescriptions from the hospital for OxyContin and asked me to help her get money so she could be free. I helped her get a new identity and gave her fair value for the pills. The next day she was gone, Hank was dead, and I was in jail. I haven't heard from

Julie Mellon

her in twenty-seven years. I always dreamed she was somewhere better. She never told me she was pregnant. Even though you look just like her, I can see Hank in your mannerisms. I figure you were what prompted her to leave in the first place."

Katie didn't like to think that she had any characteristics of a man who could beat his defenseless wife. She stopped those thoughts as Billy reached under his chair and pulled out a photo album.

"I dug this out of my attic after you was here last. Figured you might want to see some old pictures of your ma. You can take that with you if you like. The police allowed me to collect her things from the trailer where they were living after they cleaned up the crime scene. I stored them all here in the attic while I was in jail."

Katie opened the cover and saw a faded wedding picture. The bride was dressed in so many ruffles that it was nearly impossible to make out her figure. But the face that stared back at her was like looking in a mirror. Tears swam in her vision as she saw her mother for the first time in eight years.

Sarah Freeman had a list of rules for the women who stayed on her ranch. One was that once they left, they were not to return. When Katie pleaded to go to college, her mother told her that if she left, that rule applied to her as well. At eighteen, she left to go to college and hadn't been back since. Patty, the woman who helped her mother run the ranch and was responsible for taking care of all the business beyond the gates, drove her to her new apartment and helped her get adjusted. The two still exchanged letters and Katie kept her up-to-date on all that was going on in her life. She liked to envision Patty reading the letters to her mother. It made her feel connected to something in the world.

She closed the cover of the album without going any further and managed to say thank you without breaking down in tears. She stayed another hour, rocking in the rocking chair as Billy continued peeling potatoes and reminisced about his youth with Charlene. Finally, she dragged herself up, knowing she had a lot of security footage to get through that afternoon.

As she stepped off the porch, Billy asked, "Can you give this to your momma?" She turned and saw he was holding a folded piece of paper out to her. "I know you won't tell me where she is, and that's fine. But I want her to know that I still love her and that if she needs anything, I'm here."

Katie took the paper and told him she would include it in her next letter home.

Twenty-Eight

Katie was the first to show on Monday morning. While she waited for Gabi, Sheila, Michael, and Ryan she began writing on the dry erase boards in the conference room. Andy and Lucy had been called in to wrap up their most recent child pornography case. They had managed to bust open an international ring of people who were selling children online and videotaping the results for further distribution. Katie could just imagine the excitement and satisfaction they were feeling as they began the process of arresting all those involved.

Katie was trying not to let her frustration show. This case was going nowhere fast. She started making columns on the board: bookstore, fast food, department store, gym, nightclub, sporting goods store, sandwich shop, and steakhouse. As she got finished with the list, she heard Michael clear his throat behind her. She turned to see the others gathered with the expected coffee, sweet tea and donuts.

"What do you have going there?" Michael asked, handing over the Styrofoam cup of tea and a donut.

"This case isn't moving. We keep going in circles of which victim has been where. I thought writing it in black and white -- or in this case, green and red -- might help."

"Ooh, I have some of this," Gabi piped up. "I started it as

Free to Deceive

I was running through the victims' credit card statements." She pulled up a spreadsheet on her computer and began listing the names as they pertained to the various businesses.

"The bookstore only had King, Bishop, and Darden. I added Patterson there because he was a suspect at the time. But he's on the list of all the places except the gym."

Katie grabbed a blue marker and added Patterson to each list except the gym. The victim's names were in green with red headings over the columns.

Gabi resumed, "The fast food place had Bishop, Perkins, Darden, McDaniel, Rhodes and Newberry. Also Patterson and Dixon." Again, Katie added Dixon in blue. The department store had Harris, Perkins, Ellis, Darden, McDaniel, Smith, and Newberry. The gym has Ellis, Darden, McDaniel, and Edison. The club has Bishop, Darden and Rhodes, also Dixon. The sporting good store had Bishop, Harris, Perkins, Ellis, Darden, McDaniel, Edison, and Newberry. The sandwich shop had Harris, Perkins, Ellis, Darden and Rhodes. And finally the steakhouse had Harris, Porter, Ellis, Darden, Smith, Edison and Newberry. You can add Dixon to that list too."

Stepping back, they all studied the board.

"Is it sad that there were more people going to the gym than the bookstore?" Ryan asked, with a look at Katie. Katie blushed, remembering their conversation at dinner the other night and the small kiss Ryan had given her when he walked her to her room. Michael didn't miss the exchange and he wasn't very pleased with it.

There was not a single person who had been at all of the places in The Avenue. Defeated, Katie resumed her seat and grabbed a second donut.

Feeling like she was letting everyone down, Gabi added, "Well, I'm not completely finished with the credit checks. Perhaps I'll link them to more places."

Michael was the one to reassure her. "Gabi, you've done a wonderful job. Without your work we wouldn't have as much as we do. I'm sure that the break in this case will come from something you've discovered." He smiled at her to let her know he was serious.

As they began tossing around other ideas and where to go from there, an officer knocked on the door. "We just received a missing persons report. Male, 21, didn't come home last night. Thought you might be interested."

They all looked at each other. It was Monday on the first week of the month. Technically it was still June, as July 1st wasn't until later in the week. If this was related, the killer was striking early.

Free to Deceive

Katie voiced that thought. "Maybe discovering the bodies has made the person spiral?"

Michael just nodded, took the paper from the officer and all five of them, except Gabi left the room. As they headed toward the missing man's mother's home, Michael called Susanne to let her know that he was called to a possible missing persons case and would need to reschedule. Her voicemail picked up, so he left her a message saying he would come to the steakhouse later in the afternoon so they could talk when she had a break.

They pulled up to a modest ranch house to find a hysterical woman sitting with a patrolman on the front porch. Shaking off the restraining hand of the patrolman, the woman came running toward the agents as they got out of their vehicles.

"You've gotta find my son! He isn't gay. They took the wrong person. He's a good boy, please bring my son home." She collapsed in a heap, and Michael bent down and gently helped her to her feet.

"Ma'am, we need to know more about your son," Michael said. "I need you to take a deep breath and talk to me, okay?" Waving to the officer to get a glass of water, he helped her back to the chair on the front porch. The others gathered around the railing, as Michael took the second chair. They were quiet until the patrol officer came back with the water.

"Here, drink this." Michael helped her take a few sips. "Better?" At her nod, he started asking her questions as gently as possible.

"Mrs. Mason, why do you think your son is missing?"

"He isn't here!" Mrs. Mason started to get hysterical at the question. Michael jumped in to stop her reaction.

"We normally don't take missing person reports on adults until after twenty-four hours. But because of the situation, we want to make sure we act as quickly as possible. This is a standard question. Please don't take offense, just try to give me as much information as possible."

She nodded and began by giving a more detailed answer. "My son, Matt, went to the library to study last night. He's living here while he goes to school at MTSU. He should graduate at the end of the summer. He's usually late getting home, so I didn't worry. But he wasn't here when I got up this morning. I can't find him. He works at the party store in The Avenue. The news said the men that you found last week were all gay and worked at places in The Avenue. My boy isn't gay. Someone took the wrong boy."

As she was telling the story, the street began filling with media vans. Katie immediately sent the patrol officer and his partner to control the crowd. She exchanged a look with Michael and knew they were both thinking the same thing. The person leaking information had struck again, and once again, the information was not correct.

Michael refocused on Mrs. Mason. "Ma'am, the media is incorrect. The men are not all from The Avenue and they're not all gay. While we talk, is it okay for my partners to go in and have a look at Matt's bedroom?"

Receiving permission, Katie and Ryan headed inside. She had directed them upstairs to the first bedroom on the right. The room was painted a light blue with sports posters all over the walls. Matt's laptop sat on the desk, as well as a backpack filled with books.

"Seems odd for someone to go to the library without books and a computer, don't you think?" Katie asked Ryan.

Ryan came over from the other side of the room where he had been going through the closet. "Yes, it does. Not much studying going on that way."

Katie glanced out the window in time to see a male figure crossing the backyard. Pointing it out to Ryan, they took off down the stairs thinking a reporter had snuck around back.

As they reached the bottom of the stairs, the young man who was in all the pictures lining the walls stepped through the kitchen door. He stopped short at the sight of them, just as surprised as they were.

"Who the hell are you?"

"Special Agents Freeman and Brewer. We're glad to have you home, Matt. Your mother has been worried." Katie looked him over and saw no signs that he had been attacked. His bloodshot eyes and rumpled clothing reinforced her theory that he hadn't been studying the night before.

"She's been worried? Why? And why is the FBI here?"

"Perhaps you should come out to the front porch and talk to your mom." Ryan waved the young man forward and ushered him through the front door.

At the sight of her son stepping out the door, Mrs. Mason let out a scream and jumped to her feet. She grabbed him in a hug and began peppering his face with kisses mumbling, "Thank God, thank God," over and over.

"Mom, please, what's going on?"

"I thought you were kidnapped by that person who's been killing all the gays in The Avenue." It didn't matter that Michael had just told her it wasn't true, she still believed what the media said. That was how society was -- if the media said it, it must be fact.

"I'm not gay and I wasn't at The Avenue last night. Why

Free to Deceive

would I be kidnapped?"

Katie noticed that he hadn't said he was at the library. He was omitting his whereabouts without lying to his mother.

It took a while to get Mrs. Mason to calm down enough to get the story from her son. When he was finally able to talk, he told the officers that he had gone to a party at a fraternity house -- though he had said it was after the library, so his mother wouldn't think he'd lied. He'd too much to drink and did the responsible thing by staying overnight.

Finally, Michael got in his car and went to meet with Susanne as Sheila, Ryan and Katie decided to return to the precinct to take another look at the pieces of the puzzle. Katie and Sheila had giggled and refused to go with him while he interviewed the flirtatious waitress. They gave the excuse of not wanting to interfere with the lovebirds.

Twenty-Nine

Michael pulled up to the steakhouse and parked around back. It was the first truly beautiful day since all the rain last week and the parking lot was packed. He caught sight of Susanne taking an order at a table in the far corner of the restaurant. He waited until she came to put the order in the computer before speaking to her. The look on her face was not pleasant when she caught sight of him standing there.

"I don't appreciate being stood up, Agent Powell. When people make an appointment, I expect them to keep it." She began filling glasses with the requested drinks for her table.

"My apologies, Susanne. We were called to the home of a potential missing person this morning and I wanted to make sure it was handled quickly."

"I see, so the other dead men aren't as important as a new case."

Michael was surprised at her hostility. "Well, if the same person had taken this man, we wanted to try to stop him from ending up like others. So, yes a new missing person did take priority over the other thirteen."

She just harrumphed and turned to take the drinks back to the table. Glancing over her shoulder, she addressed him. "I can talk to you in ten minutes. Meet me out back so I can have a cigarette while we talk." She turned and sashayed her way across the room.

Michael hadn't ever smelled cigarette smoke on her, but then again, her perfume was so strong that it masked any other odor. Perhaps that was why she wore it. He turned and made his way through the kitchen and out the back door the employees used to come and go.

Fifteen minutes later, Susanne exited the restaurant. Michael had started sweating and had removed his jacket, careful to keep it draped over his arm to conceal his weapon. He wanted to loosen his tie, but he never presented an unprofessional appearance and the thought of doing so made him think of Dane, who always walked around with his tie loosened and the first button undone.

"Let me get my cigarettes out of the car." She led him over to a small Honda SUV and opened the hatch. Pulling her purse from the back corner, she reached in it.

Michael wasn't paying much attention to her movements, as he was watching another car pulling in and trying to visualize how the lot looked the day Franklin disappeared. He turned to ask, "Were you parked in this spot the day --"

Electricity hummed through his body and he felt his muscles

go rigid. When the pain stopped, he tried to move his arms, but his brain was no longer controlling his body. The first thing he was aware of was that he was facedown on the carpeted cargo area of the SUV. He had been tasered before during his training at the academy, so his body knew what to expect. He felt the control come back to his arms and started to lift them only to feel the electricity shoot through his body again. This time, she held the Taser in place longer.

When the pain finally receded, Michael was sweating for a different reason and was only vaguely aware of his hands being pulled behind his back. Before he could regain any control, she used zip ties to restrain his wrists and ankles. She then folded his legs behind him and hooked the wrist restraints to those on his ankles. Reaching into her pocket, she pulled out a napkin from the restaurant and stuffed it in his mouth and secured it using his tie, which she had removed from around his neck.

"Don't worry, I'll be back before the heat kills you." She brought the Taser up one more time and put it against his chest, holding it for what seemed like an eternity.

Michael didn't remember her closing the hatchback or walking away.

Thirty

Katie, Sheila and Ryan arrived back at the precinct still laughing about Michael's interview with Susanne. They had explained to Ryan why it was funny and why Katie had refused to go.

"You know, he's going to get revenge for this. You probably won't like it, either," Ryan chortled.

When they entered the room, they explained to Gabi why they were laughing and she joined in.

They put in an order for more Chinese take-out and Sheila drew the short straw to go pick it up. Meanwhile, Ryan came up with the idea of using flash cards to reorganize the information. After searching, they couldn't find index cards, so they used cut up pieces of printer paper. Labeling each with a place or person, they shuffled them around the table. Gabi continued to work on the computer, pulling whatever records she was working one.

Sheila rejoined them after returning with the food and they ate as they continued shuffling the information.

Finally, Katie looked at her watch. "It's been about three hours since Michael went to interview Susanne. Wonder what's taking so long?"

"He's probably dragging this out to make us pay for putting

him through the ordeal," Sheila giggled.

Still, Katie was uneasy. She didn't expect the usually serious Michael to play that kind of prank on her. Of course, if he hadn't found out anything, he might be dragging it out to make them think he had. She picked up her phone to call him anyway. His phone didn't even ring.

"That's strange, his phone went straight to voicemail." She hung up and tried again with the same results. Her worry increased each time she heard his message.

Gabi looked up from the computer. "Guys, we may have a serious problem."

All the attention focused on her.

"I've been running backgrounds on several of the secondary players in this case, since I haven't made any headway with the major players. I just finished with Susanne Hodgins. She made purchases at every place in The Avenue on the dates the men disappeared except the bookstore. She was also scheduled to go down the zip line the day Kelly Porter disappeared. Her parents live in Knoxville and from her records, she was in the city for the days leading up to Kelly's disappearance. She was also in Knoxville when Chad Montgomery disappeared, though I can't find a connection between them. Oh, and she lived with Dan King a few years ago."

Katie gasped. "She was the girlfriend his mother told me about. She called her Susie and described her as 'a sweet little thing.' I never put her together with Susanne."

The four of them look at each other in disbelief. Katie was the first to snap out of it, concern for her partner overriding the shock at not catching the connection days ago.

"Gabi, can you trace Michael's phone? He has GPS. We're going to head toward the restaurant. She's scheduled to work until four, so if we hurry we might catch her before she leaves."

Nodding, she switched programs to one that Andy had taught her earlier.

Sheila took the wheel because she was familiar with the streets and knew shortcuts to get them to the steakhouse faster. She had no sooner started the car than Katie's phone rang. The caller ID displayed Gabi's name.

"His phone is either turned off or the GPS is disabled. I can't find him. I have a request in to get Susanne's phone number. I'll keep trying."

Katie cursed Michael for not writing Susanne's number in the file, and then cursed herself for not going with Michael to the interview. Picking up her phone once again, she made a call to ASAC Perry informing him that Michael was missing and updating him on their suspicions. He listened quietly and then told her to keep searching while he looked into what else needed to be done.

Katie was the first out of the car when Sheila pulled up in front of the steakhouse. Sheila didn't bother to park; she just put the police placard on the dash and the three of them rushed inside. Storming their way through the restaurant, Mr. Simms met them as they entered the kitchen.

"Agents, how can I help you today?"

"We need to talk with Susanne," Katie practically interrupted his greeting.

"Susanne left early, around three. She said she wasn't feeling well."

Ryan laid a restraining hand on Katie's arm before she could rip the guy's throat out. "Do you know if she met with Special Agent Powell before she left?"

"Yes, I believe she met with him around two. She came back in and worked for another half an hour or so, but said she wasn't feeling well. To be honest, I assumed she was upset about the interview more than that she was sick. Dealing with emotional issues can be tough and we all loved Franklin."

"Can you tell us where she lives?" Sheila asked this time.

Free to Deceive

Mr. Simms went into his office and pulled up her personnel file. Writing the address down he handed it to Sheila. "Is everything all right?" His gaze kept flickering to Katie who was pacing up and down the kitchen while they were getting information.

"Agent Powell is missing and the last person we know he talked to was Susanne. We just need to talk to her and see if he mentioned going anywhere else. If you hear from her, please let me know." Sheila gave Mr. Simms her card and the three hurried back to the car.

They drove around the lot to the back of the restaurant and saw Michael's vehicle sitting in the parking lot. Ryan jumped out quickly and saw the keys and his cell phone inside.

"She won't take him to her house." Katie said.

"Why do you say that?" Neither Ryan nor Sheila was familiar with Katie's ability to read people. Ryan's question wasn't meant to second-guess her, but to ascertain why she thought so.

"She didn't take any of the others to her home. This started just after Dan King broke up with her. She's out for revenge on anyone she perceives as rejecting her. Michael cancelled their interview this morning -- he rejected her. She needs to get rid of him. Sheila, head toward Smyrna Park."

Sheila looked at Katie with her eyebrows raised. "You don't

really think she'll go back there, do you? We dug up all the others so there isn't anyone left for her to link him to."

"She's comfortable there. There's something that draws her to that spot. If she's been keeping up with this case, she would know we haven't kept surveillance on that area. It's our best hope until we get something else."

Sheila met Ryan's eyes in the rearview mirror communicating that she thought it was a ridiculous idea, but she shrugged and turned the car in that direction anyway.

Thirty-One

Sheila pulled the car to a stop just as Katie's phone rang. Grabbing it and answering without checking caller ID, Katie took off toward the pond at the back of the park from the small parking lot at the front.

"Freeman."

"It's Gabi. Susanne's phone isn't on, but her SUV has a system for tracking it. Usually, it's used for accidents and such, but I got the location of her vehicle."

Katie had stopped moving forward when Gabi called. She didn't want to be too far from the car in case they had to run to a different location. Now she stood hopping from foot to foot trying not to yell at the poor girl to just spit it out.

"Her car is on one of the back roads leading to the other side of the Smyrna Pond."

The minute the words left her mouth, Katie took off at a run toward the pond. She barely managed a 'thank you' before she hung up the phone and shoved it in her back pocket. Sheila and Ryan were on her heels.

"She's on the far side of the pond," Katie gasped.

Ryan split off from them and started circling the pond in the other direction, thinking maybe that way would get them to Michael faster.

Julie Mellon

Katie was the first to see the white SUV hidden in the trees. In a split second, she saw that Susanne had dug the trench for Michael's body, but it wasn't in place yet. She turned to see Susanne drag him out of the back of the vehicle, his arms and legs bound. His body hit the ground, but he didn't move, appearing to be unconscious.

Not breaking stride, Katie barreled into Susanne, landing on top of her as she wrestled the stun gun out of her hand. Susanne easily outweighed Katie and she fought like a wild woman. Lashing out with her foot, she caught Katie in the thigh. Katie brought her hand back and slammed it into her chin, snapping her head back and knocking her unconscious in one blow.

Ryan reached her at about that time. Looking up, she made sure Ryan would stay and finish with Susanne, then she turned and ran to Michael's side.

Susanne had already cut his clothing from his body and he lay naked and bound on the rain-softened earth. His eyes began to flutter open just as Katie reached him. Ryan draped his jacket across Michael's waist and Katie looked over to see that he had restrained Susanne, so she couldn't escape if she regained consciousness.

Seeing a pair of scissors in the back of the vehicle, Katie grabbed them and began undoing the zip ties that bound Michael.

Free to Deceive

She could hear Sheila calling in their location from a short distance away, but she didn't leave her partner.

Finally, he looked up at her with his dark brown eyes. "Don't ever make me interview a psychotic woman alone again."

He intended for his comment to be funny and lighten the situation, but he hadn't realized how Katie had berated herself for sending him alone in the first place. At his statement, she burst into tears.

"Smooth, man." Ryan said as he knelt beside Katie and put his arm around her.

Michael didn't like watching him comfort Katie, but he was still too weak to sit up, so he simply closed his eyes and squeezed her hand.

Eventually Susanne regained consciousness and Ryan left to deal with her. Shortly afterward, the ambulance pulled up and loaded Michael inside. Katie rode to the hospital with him.

At the hospital, they monitored his heart to make sure it had a steady rhythm and treated the abrasions on his wrists and ankles caused by his body thrashing around as the electric current flowed through him. He was released a few hours later with instructions to take it easy for a few days.

Just as they were releasing him, ASAC Perry arrived to make

sure he was okay.

"You didn't call my mother, did you?" Michael joked.

Perry grimaced. "No way. I learned my lesson the one time I called her after you were stabbed. It was just a flesh wound, but the entire hospital was overrun with Powells. I got an earful about how I didn't keep you safe. I don't want to repeat that if at all possible. She will never be called again until I can assess whether or not it's life-threatening."

Katie smiled, but secretly she was jealous that he had so many family members to look out for him. The thought of her own mother brought back her guilt.

"What's that look for?" he asked.

"We need to talk. But why don't we go interrogate Susanne first?"

Michael looked at her for a few minutes but finally nodded. "I think it's about time you told me what's been bothering you. Let's get this case closed."

They left the hospital and arrived at the precinct where Sheila and Ryan were waiting. Susanne had been checked out by a doctor and then processed into the prison. They had retained an attorney from the public defender's office. She was now waiting in an interrogation room.

Free to Deceive

When Michael walked into the room, Susanne began screaming at him. "You need to die, you bastard! You can't string a woman along and then just dump her the first opportunity that arises. I have feelings, you know!"

Her attorney finally got her settled down and everyone pulled seats up to the table. Susanne refused to look at Michael and angled her body away from where he sat.

Katie nodded to Sheila, allowing her to conduct the interrogation. She had the softest voice and the most compassionate personality. It took nearly two hours and many side-stories later to get the connection to all the victims.

Dan King had met her at the park the night he disappeared to tell her he was gay. It was one of the places they used to go when they dated. They would have picnics and walk the trails. In the end, he chickened out and just broke up with her. She had pushed him and he fell and hit his head on the statue of Nemesis. She panicked and buried him, taking all his clothes so no one could identify him. As she dug the hole to bury him, she felt the statue looking at her, telling Susanne that she wouldn't let him come back and hurt anyone else. Susanne didn't know that Dan was just unconscious; she'd just put his head in the water because that was how the legend of Narcissus went.

From that point on, she took those that offended her to

Julie Mellon

Nemesis as an offering to protect not only herself but other women as well.

It turned out that Chad Montgomery had signed the rejection letter to the University she had applied to. Kelly Porter had rejected her once at the steakhouse when he came to visit Keri. It was these two murders that proved without a doubt that these were not a heat-of-the-moment attacks, but rather Susanne's intent to kill.

The rest were small interactions that probably never registered with the men. Josh had helped her try on a pair of shoes and then moved on to help another woman. She perceived it as flirting with her and then rejecting her when someone else walked in. Patrick Harris had complimented her on a dress she tried on and put it on hold until she came back to get it. He wasn't on duty when she returned and she took it as a rejection. She had joined the gym as a new year's resolution, but Brian's schedule didn't allow him to become her personal trainer. When she saw him training other women, she got angry. Miles had reported her to her boss for her inappropriate flirting. Lyle had given her a free sandwich after burning the bread on the first one. She then saw him kissing his partner. Ultimately, she had just come unhinged when Dan broke up with her and the deaths were senseless killings for small perceived slights.

Free to Deceive

As the interview was winding down, so was Michael. His eyes drooped and he struggled to stay upright in the chair. Once the officer on duty escorted Susanne back to a cell, Katie assisted Michael to the conference room where they all gathered to have a small, quick celebration.

Katie excused herself and stepped into the hallway for a minute. When she returned, they all smiled and Michael got to compliment Gabi.

"I told you that something you found would break this case wide open." He couldn't help but tease her more. "But next time, please discover it before I'm kidnapped and tasered!" They all laughed and began taking down the information posted around the room.

When the room was bare of all the case materials, Katie walked Michael to the passenger side of the car and helped him in. Ryan was waiting for her by the driver's door.

"Um, so I was wondering if you might possibly be interested in going on a date?" He looked nervous and shuffled his toe against the concrete.

"Oh, um, sure. I mean, yes. That would be nice," Katie stuttered back.

He smiled as relief crossed his face. "Great. I'll let you

get your partner taken care of and I'll call you in a few days."
He reached down and hugged her, then moved to his own car.

Katie turned and watched as Sheila and Gabi faced the press to give them an update on the arrest. Sending a quick salute their way, she got in the car.

"So, you're going on a date with Ryan Brewer." It was a statement and not a question, so Katie knew he had heard their conversation.

"He's a nice guy. Nothing like his partner," Katie said defensively.

"I agree. Just be careful. I'd hate to see you get hurt."

She nodded but didn't reply.

A few minutes later, Michael sat up straight. "Where are you taking me? Why are we going to my sister's and not home? I'm tired and I don't know if I can handle all the questions from her right now."

Katie grimaced. "Well, I called your mother."

Michael let out a loud groan. "How could you do this to me? I thought you liked me."

Katie chuckled then groaned herself when she saw the number of cars in the driveway. Not only were his parents there, but every one of his seven siblings -- spouses and children too.

"Holy shit," she mumbled.

"Don't even think of trying to leave me with these people. You owe me. Besides, you're the one that called them."

"I only called your mom. I didn't know I would cause all this." She swept her hand in the direction of the front porch where no less than thirty people stood.

"In this family, we're a packaged deal. You call one, you get all. Now come help the invalid out of the car."

Michael was still experiencing moments of muscle weakness, so he put his arm around Katie's shoulders and walked with her assistance toward the porch.

He watched as his mother nudged two of his brothers toward him and before he knew it, Katie had been moved aside and he had been lifted into a chair seat formed by his brother's arms.

"Oh, come on guys. I'm perfectly capable of walking. I'm just a little weak."

They didn't listen and before he knew it, he was seated in a recliner in the living room. Everyone gathered around to hear him recount his tale. Michael saw his mother give Katie a hug and watched as she made Katie sit in a chair next to his.

The grilling from his family took longer than the interrogation of Susanne and by the time it was over, Michael felt like he was about to be hanged himself. The only positive

Julie Mellon

side was that there was a lot of food involved and every time his plate emptied, someone else refilled it.

Finally, his brothers helped him upstairs to the room he used to occupy before he bought his own house. It still had some of his clothing inside. He lay down and was asleep before his brothers closed the door on their way out.

Epilogue

The next morning, Katie drove Michael to work. She had tried to get him to take a few days off, but he refused. His only compromise was allowing her to drive. He asked her on the way in if she was still planning on telling him what was going on with her and she promised to tell him as soon as they got to the office.

Once inside the building, their coworkers surrounded him and pulled him into he break room. She took the opportunity to slip downstairs to the file room and pull the box containing more information on the Stephens murder. Michael had once told her that the file was downstairs and that it contained pictures, but she hadn't had the courage to look and verify what she already knew.

By the time she made it back upstairs, Michael was sitting at his desk with his hands folded in front of him. He watched as she sat the box on the desk and then opened her bag and pulled out the photo album Billy had given her.

Michael didn't say a word as she got herself organized.

Finally, taking a deep breath, she said, "My mother is Charlene Stephens."

About the Author

Julie is a native of Central Kentucky. After receiving her degree in English, she chose a career in higher education finance. Fifteen years later, she decided to allow her inner creative genius loose and began writing. She has been an avid reader her entire life, with a special love for mysteries, so she thought it fitting to make her first novel one of suspense. Growing up as an Army brat, she has lived in several states and foreign countries. To this day, she enjoys traveling to new places and experiencing new cultures. When at home she is likely to be found enjoying a few extreme sports, such as: rock climbing, scuba diving, or whitewater rafting. Her willingness to enter into activities of mortal peril is balanced by her commitment to ensure the quality of life for animals through her service with various dog rescue organizations. She now lives in Middle Tennessee with her three dogs, Ginny, Holly and Luna.

You can find more at: http://juliemellon.com

Or you can follow her at: https://www.facebook.com/jlmellonauthor